24 HOURS IS ALL IT TAKES

24 HOURS IS ALL IT TAKES

DAILY HABITS GUARANTEED TO CHANGE YOUR LIFE

VIVIAN RISI

MANJUL

Manjul Publishing House

First published in India by

MANJUL

Manjul Publishing House

• C-16, Sector 3, Noida, Uttar Pradesh 201301 – India
Website: www.manjulindia.com

Registered Office:
• 10, Nishat Colony, Bhopal 462 003 – India

Distribution Centres
Ahmedabad, Bengaluru, Bhopal, Kolkata, Chennai,
Hyderabad, Mumbai, New Delhi, Pune

Original English language edition published by Girl Friday Books, USA.
Arranged via Licensor's Agent: DropCap Inc.

This edition first published in 2023

Second impression 2024

ISBN 978-93-5543-342-8

Cover design: Emily Weigel

Printed and bound in India by Parksons Graphics Pvt. Ltd.

CONTENTS

INTRODUCTION

How often have you found yourself looking at someone you admire and asked yourself, *How do they do it?*

I used to wonder this myself. I'd look at people who seemed to have had ordinary opportunities and resources, but who were thriving in extraordinary ways. These people were driven and seemed to be living lives aligned with their purposes, whatever those might have been. And they seemed to be genuinely happy. They were living the best version of themselves.

What are they doing differently? What is their secret?

Flash forward many years and countless mistakes and missteps later. Through a process of trial and error (and heavy doses of discipline and drive), I now often—and very humbly—find myself on the other side of this equation as people ask me, "What's *your* secret? How do you do it?"

Everybody wants to know the secret. And once upon a time, I did too. Let's get real. A foolproof formula for success, some added edge to catapult you ahead of the pack? Who *wouldn't* want that!

So if you're interested, let's just cut to the chase and get this "secret" out into the open right now. You want to know what it is?

Ready? Lean in close. Are you listening?

The secret is . . . *crickets*.

I'm sorry to burst your bubble here, but the simple fact is—there isn't one. *Niente.* Nada. Zero. . . . There's just no secret to success. Nothing is that easy.

But here's the good news: you've already got what you need to start living your best life. Seriously! It's already within you, most of it sitting untapped, just waiting for you to call it to the surface.

Fortunately—and I know this for a fact—you've got this! How do I know? Because you've picked up this book (or tuned in to this audio recording) and sparked that first change. Obviously, you're curious about making changes, and you've turned that curiosity into action. There's no question in my mind that you're capable. So now let me ask you: Are you ready and willing to do what it takes?

Forget about "secret formulas" and shortcuts, because real, lasting change is all about putting in the work and seeing it through until positive behaviors become life-changing habits.

At any stage of life, we are all just a work in progress as we strive to better ourselves, educate ourselves, and, hopefully, experience growth along the way. It is through constantly evolving that we move forward in life, and while not every phase or evolution is necessarily the best one for us—and not every path we follow is the right one—every decision we make ultimately translates to experience that supplies us with the wisdom to help carry us into the next phase.

Imagine yourself as you are in this very moment—whatever

your situation, good or bad, and however you are feeling about your life and circumstances. Now, imagine staying at this point, in this place, forever. Seems like a pretty stale life, right? Even if things are pretty good right now, staying stuck in this spot would eventually feel like wearing cement shoes in a race while everyone else jogs past you. Life keeps happening around you, but there you are, weighed down in one spot. That's no way to live!

Because the world is ever-changing, our lives must be engaging and fulfilling if we want to thrive.

My goal here is to share what I know and motivate you to kick-start a better life, full of the things that turn your energy on and up, starting with some small but significant changes in your day. I know that you're busy; we all are. But if you're serious about living your best life, you're going to have to acknowledge one very important point from the start:

Nothing changes if *nothing changes.*

Read that again. Nothing changes—not a damn thing—if nothing changes. And it's up to each of us to create the space for change.

By now, we've established that there's no simple "recipe for success," right? This is typically the first barrier that people run into when trying to make positive changes to their lives, because the word *success* can represent so many different things to different people. What I've discovered on my journey is that how close we get to success, both in our personal and professional lives, is entirely up to us and depends on our personal definition. So here's my second key point for you to keep in mind as you explore the chapters in this book:

Success is whatever you imagine it to be.

Whether that means one day achieving your dreams as you originally envisioned them, or reimagining your goals as you go, the journey and its outcome are whatever *you* make of them. And while the possibilities really are limitless, you should start by at least generally defining what success means to you. Don't get stuck on traditional definitions of the word, or what it looks like to others. This is about you. Take a moment to consider what it is you feel you're lacking in your life. What's missing? What would complete the picture for you?

Go beyond the material *stuff*: the car you wish you drove, the extra square footage you fantasize about in your house to escape from the kids, that inground pool you're about ready to dig yourself. Go deeper and try to unearth the things of substance—feelings, accomplishments, moments of joy—that you believe you're missing out on. Make note of what comes to mind—the more specific, the better. Then set it aside for now, but keep this image handy because you will need to continue working on this as you make your way through this book.

Before we move on, I want to share a little background on how this book came to be.

In early 2019, I found myself at Indigo, Canada's leading bookstore, wandering the bookshelves for my next great read. Or to be more precise, for my next *audiobook* download. (What can I say? I'm an avid *listener.* So if my words are coming to you through headphones, or your car's Bluetooth, well, that's something we've got in common!)

Back to the story: Armed with my espresso and a little time to myself, I made my way over to my usual go-to terrain—biographies, business, and health and wellness. The store sells a lot more than books, and my route took me past displays of weighted blankets and candles. I love candles and instantly picked out a few. I nearly stopped at a satisfyingly neat stack of colorful workout gear and gadgets (I get distracted easily, and we'll circle back to how I handle this later), then reminded myself that new *books* were the focus today. I went on to explore a section of shelves dedicated to self-improvement. Finding myself in the aisle dedicated to "habit-based" books, I stopped in my tracks. Some of the covers, with their bold and commanding titles, almost shouted out from the shelves with guarantees, affirmations, and calls to action: *Best Self: Be You, Only Better*; *Take Control of Your Life*; *Change Your Schedule, Change Your Life*; *A Year of Positive Thinking*; *Breaking the Habit of Being Yourself.*

There was a habit-based angle for everyone, but this didn't surprise me. The power of habit has been a major talking point in business for as long as I can remember, and while some might brush off the importance of good habits as common sense, I am a firm believer in the power of habit in the sense that it can offer both motivation and positive reinforcement. I also believe in the power of shared experience, whether it comes from a book, a podcast, or a person at a live event. All that wisdom and energy from others has proven effective and deeply impactful for me.

My first foray into the world of motivational wisdom was back in the early 1990s, still relatively early in my career. I was working as a real estate sales agent at one of my very first brokerages when opportunity came knocking. Literally.

A young man who identified himself as a "road rep" came into the office to promote an upcoming motivational event featuring a fresh voice on the scene: Tony Robbins. At first, that name sounded unfamiliar to me, but then the rep described Tony as a captivating young man with a towering build, booming voice, and inspiring backstory. Larger than life. Okay, now this sounded familiar. I *had* heard of him as someone who had been gaining a lot of traction in the business world for his thunderous persona, animated delivery, and innovative concepts.

"Do you want to change your business for the better—and change your life?" the rep asked.

Of course I did! Who would say no to that? The rep's strategy was simple but effective; he was asking me a question he already knew the answer to. My interest was definitely piqued.

But with Tony Robbins's rising popularity, tickets to one of his events were pricey. I was a single mother with three kids and a business in sales that already had me scrambling to keep it all afloat. I had to prioritize, and between food, rent, and the other necessities of keeping a family going on a single income, tickets to this event didn't really qualify as a *necessity.*

I told the road rep I was too busy to attend even though it was really a lack of *funds* that was at issue here. But as he persisted, I finally confessed the real reason.

"I can't afford to go."

And then—and I'll never forget this, because this is what got me—he looked me dead in the eye.

"Lady, you can't afford *not* to go!"

That did it. He had found the right match to ignite a fire somewhere inside, and I began to waver. I *wanted* to go. And something in my gut—in my core—told me I *should* go. I *needed* to be at this event. Because, really, what was standing between me going or not going was money: I didn't have the money to go, but if this event lived up to the promoter's claims, it could end up sparking real, positive change in my way of thinking and my life overall. I decided he was right; I couldn't afford *not* to go.

I took a chance and paid for a ticket I couldn't afford on a credit card that was already at its limit. I was excited, but I also felt guilty. Had I just agreed to something that was selfish and irresponsible with money I didn't have?

I stewed about my decision until the day of the event. That morning, I followed my usual routine while the anticipation built inside, and after dropping my kids off at school, I rushed to the venue, eager to find a seat and catch my breath.

No such luck. After presenting my ticket and pushing open the doors to the event space, I discovered it was a sold-out show and, being one of the last to arrive, I was shuffled over to the standing-room-only section. I settled into an open pocket of space and tried to center myself, knowing I needed to be as present as possible. Every dollar spent on this ticket was a dollar taken away from my family, and I couldn't afford to miss a moment.

When Tony Robbins took to the stage, he somehow, even in this massive space packed full of people, engaged and connected with each and every one of us. As he shared his backstory, his lowest points, and the pivotal moments that helped propel him onto the path he was on now, I was completely locked onto his every word. For me, it wasn't about where he was now—the success and flash and fame; it was about where he had come *from*. He was a living, breathing example of an important truth: Where you start from doesn't matter. It only matters that you *start*.

I had walked into this experience, hoping for the best. I had been optimistic—but I was also tired. I'd been working so hard to keep it all together, worrying constantly, not so much for myself as for my children. I was physically and mentally exhausted. I was also carrying a lot of shame and guilt throughout my day, feeling as though I'd robbed my kids of stability and security because I hadn't been able to keep our family together. I think most people who've gone through separation or divorce can agree that, warranted or not, there's a lot of guilt around feeling like you've "broken" your family apart—when in fact, we are often making hard choices with the best of intentions. I spent so much of my energy just putting one foot in front of the other, doing my best for the people who relied on me, and it was only in hindsight that I realized I'd been carrying this bag of bricks into every room I walked into. Bricks of fatigue and shame and guilt and worry. Heavy bricks.

But that spark that brought me to the event now became a burning fire, igniting hope and energy. No miracle had been performed. No magic potion had been passed around. Tony hadn't offered an instant fix to all my problems. But after absorbing the electric energy bouncing off every wall in that meeting space and taking in the powerful words spoken, I found that my perspective shifted just enough to allow me to remove a few bricks from my bag, which in turn boosted my inner strength. I came away believing I was not a bad person. I was not a loser. The bad things in my life's story did not define me, and I would no longer let my past troubles handicap me from moving into my future.

My mindset also shifted at some point between walking into that sold-out event and walking out. *What is so different between the positive, successful man on stage and me?* We both woke up with the same number of hours in the day, and neither of us had been cut any breaks along our journeys. No, Tony didn't have the trademark on a secret sauce. *I* could do this. I could make some real changes. I could build a world of stability for my family, achieve my career goals, and really live a life aligned with my purpose—and it would start with a new mindset of growth, positivity, and confidence.

But the story doesn't end there. You want to talk about manifesting? Life really does come full circle. What if I told you that, over twenty years later, I found myself at another Tony Robbins show? Only this time . . . I was on stage with him!

I had been invited to introduce him at one of his sold-out motivational speaking events in Toronto. And when the day came, I found myself looking out at the crowd, a sea of five thousand eager attendees, all looking up at the stage from where I had once stood myself. What a surreal moment! But of course, as life happens, the scheduled plan for my brief introduction went out the window when the emcee slipped me a note. I glanced down at the piece of paper atop the podium while bright spotlights beat down from overhead. The man of the hour was stuck in city traffic!

A few rehearsed words of introduction suddenly became an impromptu retelling of my very first Tony Robbins show, and how I'd trusted my gut and found a way to pay for my ticket to one of the most powerful events of my life. I told the crowd that, even after all this time, and the many impactful experiences I've had since attending that very first show, I will never forget how powerful and inspiring it was to hear Tony's story, relate to his struggle, and walk out of that experience committed to making real changes in my life too. I explained that it wasn't that he reinvented the wheel; it wasn't even just his message. It was his *delivery* and his positive reinforcement of the need for daily change and growth. That was what made the difference for me.

And in the funny way in which life often unfolds, it was my time onstage that day that would eventually prompt me to write my first book. *Yes You Can: It All Starts with You* shares my tried-and-true life lessons to not only encourage people to make changes in their lives, but to help them recognize their inner power and spark the motivation to get started on their own path of purpose.

But another book was waiting in the wings; I just didn't know it yet until I began to study all those bookshelves displaying self-help titles centered on habitual behaviors and the value of routines. As it turns out, I'm definitely a creature of habit. This doesn't mean I don't leave room for flexibility in my day. Of course I do! In a business where things are always coming up, I have to be able to adapt as I go. But solid habits and effective routines have *always* been the foundation on which I frame my days. The trick is figuring out which habits will work for you, and then implementing them effectively and successfully.

Some of the habit-based books at Indigo promised to change your life in twenty-one days. Some teased that a single habit could make the difference in just a year. And so on. What many of them had in common, I noticed, was that they required major time commitments from the reader, from several consecutive days of repetition required to master a new habit to several weeks or even *months* of commitment.

On the one hand, I got it: good things take time, and adopting new habits does take consistency. No arguments there.

But, I wondered, *can there be another way to elicit change? To inspire positive shifts without making people feel added pressure or the demand of more time commitments in their lives? Can there be another way to tap into true, positive change?*

After a few weeks, these thoughts were still floating around in my mind until one day I found myself seated across from a new colleague on our team, who asked me that same old question.

"How do you get so much done in a day? You're always smiling; you always seem positive and energetic. You're the CEO of a company; you have three kids, six grandkids, elderly parents who rely on you. And I *know* you're always so busy with work! How do you manage it all?"

Well, first of all, I wanted to say, *I'm only human, although being an optimist helps. Even so, things aren't always perfect. Some days are rough; what can I tell ya? That's life!* As I was trying to formulate a reply that was honest, real, and—hopefully—inspiring, a light bulb clicked on. It was time for me to share my wisdom with more than just a few colleagues here and there. It was time to write a book about *my* "24"—my everyday habits and routines.

It's not that I consider my approach to habits and daily routines to be the best and only way to do things. Nor do I believe that my insights trump the suggestions offered by other experts out there. It's simply what has worked for *me* and what has propelled me from my role as a struggling single parent to becoming the president of one of North America's largest realty brokerages, where I oversee more than fourteen hundred sales representatives and employees. Daily habits and routines are also what helped me enjoy a fulfilling personal life as a daughter to my inspiring parents (both in their nineties and thriving!), a proud mother to three amazing (all-grown-up) children, a grandmother to six incredible young people, a devoted partner, and a friend to those who keep me smiling—and sane! So if my advice can help even *one* person out there who wants to make some real change, in a realistic and significant way, then every ounce of effort put into these pages will have been worth it.

I encourage you to explore this book the way I approach each day: one hour at a time. And the only commitment I ask from you is your willingness to try my recommended habits and attitudes for a single day. Just one day. Starting tomorrow! I guarantee you'll be able to see and feel the benefits of these positive routines right away, no matter which ones you start with.

Listen; I know it's not easy to change your perspective, and changing your way of thinking about a few daily habits won't suddenly make your life problem-free—no, no, no! That's not how this works! But if you're willing to open your mind to some new ideas, and if you're patient enough to reconsider some things you already know, but from another angle, you're going to benefit. Will there be some work involved on your part? Of course! But that's another key motto of mine:

Change happens just outside your comfort zone.

That's where you see the results!

As you read, think about your 24-hour day as having a beginning, a middle, and an end, just like that novel on your bedside table. Unless you have a reversed work or sleep schedule, your beginning likely takes place in the morning and your ending is likely in the evening. I've generally organized this book, and my corresponding recommended habits, based on this circadian cycle, emphasizing some habits that work well, at least for me, in the morning and some that work best at the end of the day. But there is no absolute rule about when most of these routines should be implemented; the most important consideration is what works for you.

Positive, productive, and realistic habits are going to be the keystone behaviors that carry you through your day and into your best future. They are going to position you optimally for success and opportunities beyond your wildest dreams. But before these amazing things can find their way into your orbit, you need to do the work. You have to shift your perspective and make some tough decisions now so that you can reap the benefits later.

Still skeptical? I hear you. But think of it this way: if someone can offer you the chance to change your life for the better *tomorrow,* isn't that worth having an open mind *today*? Remember: it's better to jump than fall, so take charge and leap into change!

HABIT 1

OWN YOUR MORNINGS, AND YOU'LL OWN THE DAY

"Either you run the day, or the day runs you."

—Jim Rohn

They say you can never buy more time . . . but what if I could show you how? What if, with just one small change per day, I could help you add an extra *two weeks* of waking time to your life, every year?

You can do that simply by waking up and getting out of bed!

That's right: just stop hitting the snooze button, and get that brain and body into motion. Toss those covers right off, swing those feet over the bedside, and pull yourself up into a standing position. Take a swig of that water bottle on your night table. How do you feel? I realize you might feel a little cranky. Your eyes might still be sensitive to the light. You might feel a bit chilled now that you've gotten your butt out of your cozy bed. And you might even be a little annoyed by my cheerful morning tone. (Yes, I guess I can be a *little* annoying at times, but hang in there. You'll grow to love me—and all the extra time I find for you.)

Getting up early is your first step in the right direction, and it's the most basic example of how you can make a positive change in your life every day. It may feel small, but that first action makes an impact. So good morning! You're alive. It's a new day. And it's going to be a great one because you've already started to make some real changes in your life by getting out of bed early.

To be honest, I think I've always been a bit of an early bird as far as mornings are concerned. My parents tell the story of how, in my youngest years, I'd wake up before everyone else and busy myself "tidying" the kitchen. As you can imagine, I was probably making more of a mess than cleaning up, but as the story goes, I was devoted to this little ritual for extra time. I guess I felt like I wanted to start the day with some small achievement, something worthy of praise from my parents, a contribution to our little world within those walls. Even in these younger years, I was conscious that we didn't have much. My parents were humble and hardworking immigrants who gave us everything they could. Little gestures like tidying up the kitchen were how my younger self found a way to "give back."

I truly believe that morning time is sacred. I wake up with the birds each day, and as I open the blinds and take in whatever the outside world is offering as the sun comes up, I'm reminded of a holiday in Rome I took some years ago. Of all the sights and sounds and, of course, incredible foods I indulged in during that trip, the most impactful lasting memories for me were the mornings. I would rise with the sun and open the shuttered, wooden balcony doors that gave way to the world below. At this time of day, Rome was not yet busy with honking cars and street vendors that would soon overtake the roads and sidewalks. The tourists were still asleep in their beds, no clicking cameras or open maps to guide them through the cobblestone paths. No, at that moment, as the sun began to illuminate every inch of this incredible cityscape, it was just myself on the balcony and the street-sweepers below, priming the landscape for the usual day's chaos ahead. I would stand there as the minutes ticked by, and little by little, all of Rome would come to life, the city opening up before my eyes. And it's this experience that I brought home with me: this sensation of rising with the day, the power in seizing that moment and being part of that exclusive window of time that so many people miss out on.

The European scenery is spectacular, of course, but you can't rely on vacations to capture this spirit. You need to find this sense of daily connection from wherever you are. In my everyday life, I seize this first habit of the day from wherever I start my morning, whether that's at my home in the city or on the cottage deck by the water. All you need is yourself and a view or a spot outdoors. The morning sun rises no matter where you are—so there's no excuse to miss the moment!

This time for me is crucial. It's become a part of who I am.

The hourglass of life resets every day, every 24 hours. That's all we get, God willing, for as long as we have on this earth. We're all gifted with this same valuable, nonrenewable resource from the moment we open our eyes: 24 golden hours to use and spend as we choose. Remember: you will never again be as young as you are in this moment, right now, which means every minute in front of you is precious. The day belongs to you!

In all areas of our lives, we need to learn to value quality over quantity, and that begins, literally, at the start of our day, when our mornings set the tone for all the hours ahead. What kind of "morning person" are you? Does the quality of *your* morning measure up to what you deserve? Do you relate to that perky morning news anchor who's practically jumping through your screen, or are you more the "don't even look at me until I have my coffee" type?

The proverb about the early bird getting the worm speaks to the idea that getting an early start helps maximize the potential for a positive outcome for all your tasks throughout your day. Habitual early birds, who see the value in seizing the day before the rest of the world, are on autopilot from the moment they wake up. Their eyes open, their brains click on, and their subconscious minds kick into gear. They're rarely groggy. They step into the next phase of their day *alert*. And they're also not as rushed as everyone else around them. Everything unfolds from there like a choreographed dance.

At this point in my life, I have no need for an alarm clock. My body is so in sync with my routine that I naturally wake up at the same early hour each day. But this is also in large part because the rest of my day follows a general rhythm that carries me into my sleep time at a routine hour, which then allows me to keep my morning routine stable.

The way I see it, when I wake in the mornings—whether it's as the sun rises or in total darkness (fellow Canadians can testify to our dark winter months!)—I own the day, baby! I look out my window for that first view of my 24, and I feel myself bonding to the day. Whether I'm watching the sun rise or living out the night's last legs of darkness as it makes way for the light, I can actually feel myself syncing up in tandem with the day. This early start is empowering. It feels as if I'm claiming an advantage over the day before it even begins.

I recall a conversation I had with a very successful businessperson many years ago. He, too, was an early riser. His motivations for waking up were centered on the ability to "get ahead" of the day and, in effect, set the tone as a leader in his role. Up early, he would steam ahead full force, visiting his active work sites before the official start of the workday and taking inventory of each project, its status, and any issues or items that would need to be addressed. He would give himself the assurances of the projects' progress, and the state of the area, affording him the confidence of being on top of things before his teams and laborers reported for work. As a leader for his business, he knew the onus was ultimately on him to ensure that his people were working on a safe site, that the updates he was passing along were accurate, and that he knew firsthand how things were going. There were minimal surprises for him once the day began because he had used his morning to get out in front of his day.

I like to think his practice applies to showing leadership at home, too. Parents are generally the first to rise, setting up themselves and their families for the day ahead. And I think it's safe to say that those of us who are able to carve out that extra time in the mornings feel less like we are "catching up" with the herd come 9:00 a.m., when the rest of the world seems to "clock in." It's an advantage that depends on many variables in your life, sure, but it's one worth aspiring to in whatever way you can.

The early bird enjoys a private relationship with the world that really sets the pace for the rest of the day.

That private morning moment—the early rise and connection with the day ahead: it's this first habit that makes all the difference for me.

This is what you'll come to discover, once you find habits and routines that work for you, and how to make the most of your 24 hours. You won't go back. I'm betting most of you would agree that what you're doing now isn't working. Or at the very least, you can agree that things could definitely be better.

So why not commit to one day of change? Small shifts that you can implement into your next set of 24, free of charge and with a guarantee for change. What have you got to lose?

I'm not alone in promoting this habit. Robin Sharma is a former-lawyer-turned-bestselling-author-and-motivational-speaker who firmly attests to its power in his book *The 5AM Club*. "Winning starts at your beginning," he writes. "Own your mornings, and you'll master your life."

There are many reasons why he, and so many of the world's other foremost motivational figures, suggest waking up early as a keystone to success. One is that it works. Another is that you never know what's coming. Picture this: The phone rings. *Ring—ring—rinnnnnng!* You answer it and hear an ominous voice.

"Hello, this call is to inform you that you'll be expiring in a few months. Have a great day!"

I wake up every day, both on the good days and on the not-so-good ones, grateful for every drop of life I get to live. And that's why I jump out of bed in the mornings. Okay, maybe some mornings it's less of a jump and more of a slow pour, but even so, I am truly *excited* about my life and the opportunity to take on the day, to make a difference, to help people, and to live my purpose. To make the most of this gift of 24 hours. And while no one likes to think that their time may be up anytime soon, it's important to remember that this gift of time isn't on some guaranteed subscription service forever. Everything has an expiry date, and every day is a blessing.

Are you ready to make a commitment to try out a new habit, not to me—we've only just met—but to yourself?

ACTION ITEM #1: SET TOMORROW'S ALARM TO RING AN HOUR EARLIER THAN USUAL.

Yes, do it tomorrow—not sometime in the future. It's just one morning I'm asking for here, and this won't be that hard. After all, you're not committing yourself to this change for a month, or even a week. We're only talking about one day, just to try it out. So punch your new wake-up time into your phone, write it down on a notepad, and reset your alarm now to lock this plan for a new habit into place starting tomorrow. Done? Awesome!

Savor this moment, because you've just taken an idea and turned it into an action—and it feels good, doesn't it? I'm confident that when you wake up an hour early tomorrow, you'll see and feel the shift, and you'll be hooked. This little change will translate to fifteen amazing bonus days over the course of the next year—and it will inspire you to act on the *next* change in your daily routine. So read on!

HABIT 2

PLAN AHEAD, BUT PREPARE TO PIVOT

"Intentional living is the art of making our own choices before others' choices make us."

—Richie Norton

Let's start this one off with a little survey. How many of the following can you relate to? (Check all that apply.)

- "There's never enough time!"
- "How is it already ______ o'clock?"
- "I feel like I haven't gotten anything done."
- "Where has the day gone?"

If you're like most people, you have sometimes started

your day already feeling as though you're ten steps behind everyone else. Or you've found yourself rushing from one task to the next in a frenzy, feeling as though the day is passing you by in a blur. The good news? This common, haunting feeling of never having enough time is fixable. It's true; I promise! And here's how.

Live with *intention*.

You're going to be seeing that word a lot throughout this book because it's one of my fundamental personal principles. I live my life, down to every hour of my daily 24, with intention: the intention to be present, to enjoy the moment, to make a difference, to live my purpose. My intentions are endless, and they represent my driving force at every step. They're what keep me from wasting time watching television in the morning, or scrolling mindlessly through social media, or pouring *another* cup of coffee. None of these easy activities gives me any real payoff in my day to come, and my ultimate goal is always to maximize my mornings, and in effect, maximize my whole day. So I rely on intention as the foundation for my day's plan, which in turn positions me optimally and guarantees the best-case scenario for my next 24. This is a deal breaker for me—an absolute must.

Motivational speaker Jim Rohn advised to "never begin the day until it is finished on paper." That means aligning yourself with the present and consciously reflecting on what lies in front of you. Sometimes planning involves finding a quiet spot, sitting still, shutting your eyes, and envisioning yourself going through the physical motions of your day as called for by your intentions. Or maybe it's just doing a ten-minute scan of your schedule, reading your appointments aloud, and pausing at each one to try to manifest your desired outcomes. For some, the daily planning process might even include a vision board, where, after reviewing your schedule for the day, and keeping in mind your ultimate goals and purpose, you turn to your board and visually identify the direct link between the actions planned for today and the end results you are planning for the future.

Remember: good habits and routines are all about consistency, so find what method works for you and go from there. This isn't a one-size-fits-all strategy; don't be afraid to try a few different techniques before settling on the one that feels right to you. Whatever it takes, this habit is crucial to the rest of your day because, in doing this, you're taking control of your time and getting a jumpstart into the day. It's also better than going in blind, because—let's be realistic here—the unexpected will happen. When it does, you'll be able to anchor yourself to the moment and pivot if you have a plan to work from.

That word, *pivot,* is a key element in this second habit. You can never plan for everything, even with the best intentions. The unknown will always be there waiting for you. That's just life. The motto for the television series *Survivor* comes to mind: *Expect the unexpected.* It always amazes me to think that people all over the world, from all kinds of backgrounds, dream of being cast on a TV show where the whole premise is to be left stranded outside of your comfort zone. A remote island with the bare basics. Grueling physical and mental challenges.

And, oh yeah, a whole batch of strangers bitching and biting at each other's heels for a chance at the grand prize. As if real life weren't enough of a grind!

But then I consider "real life," and it's not hard to see the parallels: finding yourself outside your comfort zone, diving into the unknown, and challenging yourself. In that context, I can see the appeal; *Survivor* is, in some ways, real life on a much larger scale. I won't be applying to be cast on the show anytime soon, but to some degree, I get it.

Being able to pivot starts with expecting that things won't go according to plan. Some people thrive in the unknown whereas others dread it, but we all find ourselves there at one point or another. When that happens—when the plan goes up in smoke—what do *you* do? Roll over? Throw your hands up and admit defeat?

No way. Not an option. You *pivot* and you find your way back on course.

In the early spring of 2021, I was at the tail end of a day like any other. Okay, yes, the world was in the middle of a global pandemic, but at that point we had safety protocols in place and everyone was doing their best. As much as it could be, life was business as usual.

I'd woken up that morning—early as always—and I took in the sunrise while drinking my smoothie after a quick workout. I went into the office and, being in my element, dove into the workday: a mix of scheduled Zoom meetings, check-ins with my agents and staff, and as always, a few unplanned fires to put out. It was pretty much business as usual. I closed out the day around 6:00 p.m. and headed home.

The funny thing about life is that, as much as we'd like some advance warning, there's never a big, flashing sign letting us know we're about to have the rug pulled out from under us. So there I was at home that evening, following my regular routine, until I suddenly found myself being transported to the hospital in an ambulance. After several tests and frustrating periods of time spent grappling with the unknown and waiting for some real answers, I eventually learned that I would have to undergo a hysterectomy.

I knew this was a time to pivot. Moreover, I *wasn't* going to feel sorry for myself. No way! I'd been blindsided, sure. No one is invincible, no matter who you are. People often look at me as a strong and powerful woman—a tough "lady boss"—but that day, out of the blue, life knocked me off my feet. And from one day to the next after that, tests and treatments became a part of the "new normal" for me. Life was certainly throwing me for a loop, but I wasn't about to roll over and let this health scare take over my life entirely.

Pivoting didn't mean throwing my routine out the window. In fact, I tried to stick to it as much as possible. My routine kept me sane and grounded during such a surreal period of my life. But there were times when I had to veer away from my usual routine. I did my best to modify it in a way that would still work for me, trying not to cut things out if I could avoid doing so while penciling new activities and commitments into my days. My early mornings were still mine, so I was grateful for the ability to keep that ritual in play, but it was a shock to the system to feel as though I had lost some control over my own body—one I had spent most of my adulthood taking good care of. On days when my energy levels would dip, for example, I had to find the strength to accept my current circumstance and adjust in response to the signals my body was giving me. This was especially true after my surgery. And while my instincts during that time were to push through the discomfort and get back to being "me," I was humbled by the realization that the body talks, and while the mind might be ready and willing to get up and go, the body sometimes makes that decision for you.

When I got my diagnosis, I knew that I was just one of many women who had been handed the same news, and I also knew that I was fortunate in more ways than not. Finally armed with some answers, I started mapping out next steps, setting out a plan for my pre-op, my surgery, and my post-op time as I would normally do with anything else. I had a plan, but I still ended up having to pivot. My time, my body's reaction to the process, my day-to-day personal life and business—all of it required a new level of consideration and navigation. Suddenly, scheduling myself became a little trickier. Would I have an appointment at the clinic that day? How would I be feeling? There were new variables in the mix, and pivoting meant making the adjustments where they were needed—planned or not.

And I've gotta say, I did a pretty good job of keeping it all together. I did my absolute best, anyway. It wasn't easy, but it wasn't *impossible,* and what I stayed focused on were my intentions. It just so happened that now I had to incorporate a new intention into my daily routine: navigating an unexpected health issue.

So why spend so much time preparing and reviewing plans if life is going to throw you curveballs anyway?

I'll tell you why. When you wake up with intention, plan to make the most of your day, and align yourself to your purpose, you are setting a path with confidence. That way, when shit happens—and it will, folks—you'll know what direction to lean into. Looking at it another way, think of your daily plan as the GPS route for your day, and then unexpected things arise and force you to take detours. Do they temporarily throw you off course? Sure they do. But do they demand that you give up on your destination altogether? No way! Pivoting doesn't necessarily mean you go off in an entirely new direction. Sometimes it means small shifts. Or it might just be a matter of taking a moment—breathing, counting one, two, three, or as many counts as it takes to center yourself—and then getting back to your overall plan. If you don't know where you're heading or your general route for getting there, an unexpected detour can really derail you. But detours are a lot less frightening when you've got a plan.

Mapping out your route each day helps you stay on track—or get back on track when life takes you on detours.

Trust me, you'll be hooked on that added sense of confidence if you have a plan before you need to pivot. Just imagine feeling prepared as you head into each day, knowing where you're going, and then being able to tackle the day's hurdles with the energy you generated while setting your intentions. And managing the unexpected with clear, calm, and collected thoughts!

Often, people struggle with the habit of planning because it's just one more thing to merge into their schedules. They can't seem to find the right time for this activity. Well, let me tell you something. When it comes to any new habit, there's never going to be the right time to start, because this is real life, and there's always going to be something that happens and interferes with the plan. You have to *make* the time and *commit* to this new habit—and to every other change you're making in your life.

Some people think that, instead of coming up with a detailed plan, it's just easier to avoid the unexpected, or deny its possibility, until it's right in front of their faces. And okay, this might feel easier in the moment. But is it smarter? Sorry—nope! Although it happens to all of us every now and then—a bad day, a rough week, a crisis with the kids, some family emergency, the car, the job, a sore spot in our schedule—and we wish we could just avoid the problem altogether, we can't live that way. If you find yourself living in denial and avoidance, you need to dig deep and start asking yourself some real questions about what drives you so hard to avoid potential problems. That hesitation is a signal from your inner voice, telling you that something is up; it's a warning sign, like a construction worker on the highway, waving an orange flag to alert you to the detour ahead. You need to get to the root of what the issue is and face it head-on, always coming back to your intentions, and then get back to work on your plan, making whatever changes you need to make.

Every day—every single day—is a gift, and it can be hard to keep that in mind when times are tough and schedules get complicated. But you're alive and breathing. And life is happening now. This isn't a dress rehearsal. It's the real deal. So let's work on your plan for tomorrow!

ACTION ITEM #2: TAKE TEN MINUTES TO REVIEW YOUR INTENTIONS FOR THE DAY AND IDENTIFY OPPORTUNITIES FOR FLEXIBILITY IN THE EVENT YOU NEED TO PIVOT.

Fix what needs fixing so that someday soon, you'll begin waking up and feeling good about your life. Because you only have one shot at it, and every set of 24 is a gift, not a guarantee. Don't waste this daily gift. Prepare for it; be present; pivot when necessary and live it to its fullest potential.

The open highway awaits! What better time than now to plan your route?

HABIT 3

EMBRACE YOUR DAILY RITUALS

"We become what we repeatedly do."

—Sean Covey

Now that you've awakened early and centered yourself for what lies ahead, it's time for the next step in making the most of your day.

Think of your favorite novel, or television show, where the important characters are introduced early on, and seemingly irrelevant plot points and specific details are dropped into the mix like seeds to be nurtured and grown. By the end, the whole story will come together because of those details that were presented early on. Similarly, the beginning of your day sets the stage for everything. This is where you plant the seeds and make those first specific moves.

If you were to make a list of the little things you do each morning, including all your seemingly insignificant daily rituals, what would that list look like? My list of little things, which I do each morning on autopilot, serves as the groundwork that keeps me aligned with my purpose, regardless of the surprise twists and occasional bumps in the road.

We tend to dismiss these little rituals as meaningless—just something we're in the habit of doing. We drink a protein smoothie, fill our thermos with filtered water, and take the same route to work every day. No big deal, right? Wrong! Everything we do matters. Everything. And the key to remember here is that the little rituals matter *over time.*

We get into trouble when, in the interest of short-term convenience, we overlook the importance of small details and their relationship to our long-term goals. We may reach for those sugary, processed treats at the office because we need to satisfy our immediate hunger if we don't make those protein smoothies at home. We go straight for the coffee because we need an instant pick-me-up, instead of drinking ice-cold water. We check our phones as we rush through traffic because we indulged in that extra bit of sleep and were late leaving the house.

When we fall off our routines and wind up depriving our bodies of proper nourishment and hydration or adding undue stress and risk to our mornings, all in the name of short-term satisfaction, we trigger what could become a pattern of self-indulgent behaviors with immediate payoff but long-term, lasting penalties. Studies have shown that the little things at the start of your day have the greatest impact on your day as a whole.

Former US Navy SEAL and admiral William H. McRaven writes about this in his book *Make Your Bed: Little Things That Can Change Your Life . . . and Maybe the World.* He suggests that little habits like making your bed are directly related to successfully navigating through life's challenges because they establish a pattern of completing tasks. While delivering the commencement speech at the University of Texas in 2014, he advised that accomplishing that small task in the morning instills pride, encourages us to do more, and reminds us that the little things count and, in a sense, represent stepping-stones to greatness. As McRaven so famously suggested, "If you want to change the world, start off by making your bed." Powerful stuff!

Bestselling author Charles Duhigg takes the concept of making your bed a step further in *The Power of Habit: Why We Do What We Do in Life and Business.* He comments that the simple action of making your bed may not result directly in increased productivity in the workplace, but he considers it a "keystone habit" that can make way for other habits to stick also.

Whether we're talking about making a bed, doing some yoga stretches, or checking in with our partners, healthy morning rituals can take time to develop and to have noticeable impact, and this usually involves some trial and error, as we work to figure out, step by step, what works best for each of us. What differentiates those who establish, and maintain, these successful morning rituals?

Intention, planning, and consistency.

Your outfit for the next day won't lay itself out the night before. That healthy smoothie won't blend itself, and that roadblock that has you stuck for an extra fifteen minutes *every morning* won't resolve itself. In the same way that making your bed means you need to have sheets and comforters and pillows at the ready, you might need to pick out your clothes for the next day before you go to bed, keeping in mind whatever your intention might be—comfort, professional image, and so on. You might need to prep and wash your berries and kale and toss them into the blender the night before if your intention is to get out the door fast the next day. And if you know you need to get to work on time, don't keep using the excuse of "There's so much traffic!" That may work once, but come on! Once you know from experience that traffic may hold you up, be proactive and plan an alternative route—just in case tomorrow is another big roadwork day. Be smart and take preventative measures. In other words, paying attention to the little things means more than just noticing them.

You need to make the little things work for you as part of your daily plan.

It takes commitment. But where to start?

To be effective, your morning rituals need to surround things that you naturally gravitate toward. There's no reason to force yourself to adopt behaviors that you wouldn't normally be drawn to—why make it harder on yourself? You might be tempted, for example, to get overly ambitious and create a routine based on ideals: set your alarm for five o'clock, map out an extensive workout routine, and gulp down a smoothie full of greens you absolutely hate. All those things are great morning ritual ideas, and they might be on the path of self-improvement that speaks to you. But if it means you're trying to become someone other than who you are, you need to stop and find what *works for you.*

When we set our goals on the idea of "becoming someone else," we set the bar at a level that immediately seems out of reach. You're working toward becoming someone new, and that can feel impossible. And for good reason. Have you ever tried spending the day being someone other than yourself? Every action feeling forced, every move requiring the maximum effort and energy. Whew! No wonder so many people give up before they even begin! Just thinking about it is exhausting.

Remember, when working toward self-improvement, you should focus on exactly that: *self*-improvement—maximizing the potential and performance of the person *you already are.* In my first book, *Yes You Can,* I addressed the idea that your journey toward personal success is not *one size fits all*! The same applies to your daily routines and rituals. So when you're ready to get serious about changing your life for the better, plan changes that offer the path of least resistance and align themselves with your natural rhythm. Listen to your body. Let your natural instincts guide you. And keep it simple.

Thinking about my own morning routine, I realized that my rituals have become so second nature to me that every step of my routine just flows naturally. I start with rising early to work out, which sometimes means just dropping to a mat on the floor and doing a quick twenty-minute yoga flow. All movement is movement, after all, and I find that by leaving little "traps" for myself, like setting a yoga mat within sight and reach, I give myself zero room for excuses not to get moving. Some other early rituals include whipping up healthy smoothies and walking my dog, Skye. It's all just a daily part of my life. And you can bet each of these "autopilot" actions contributes positively, in some way, to both my morning and the day to follow. Working out provides me with the endorphins and adrenaline to really hit the ground running. My vitamin-rich smoothie supplies me with nourishment for my body and mind—not to mention healthy fuel to carry me until the lunch hour. Even a quick walk outdoors or tossing the ball for Skye offers the "me time" I need to enjoy my loving and furry friend and take in that first breath of fresh air, watching her excitement as she fetches the ball, setting my mood in the right place for a busy day ahead.

In my daily life, some of the "little things" that have evolved into foundational nonnegotiables in my day include social rituals. And while I have several morning rituals that work really well for me, one of my favorites is lunch!

I never used to have much of a lunchtime routine. At the

start, I'd find I'd either get too busy and reach for something easy like a granola bar—or I'd skip it altogether. And eventually, realizing I needed some form of fuel to carry me through the rest of the day, I started going out for lunch. I guess this is a pretty basic midday routine for those of us who work out of business offices, but it started to drive me a little nuts. Going out meant I'd have to make time to stop whatever it was I was doing (I'm sure many of you can relate to not having a "defined" lunchtime!), get in my car, drive someplace nearby, get seated, wait for my food—and, inevitably, be delayed in coming back because I'd end up seeing someone I knew and wind up chatting with them. It started to become a pain. I love food and I love people, but this just wasn't working for me as an everyday thing. But neither was skipping lunch altogether—or banking on a granola bar to sustain me. So I started ordering take-out lunch. A tasty chicken salad from a local restaurant became my go-to. But even that eventually got problematic. I'd find myself halfway through my salad, with people coming in and out of my office, and I'd start to feel bad that I only had one order and not much left over to share. I still hadn't found a lunch routine that was hitting the mark for me.

That was when I started planning ahead, bringing fresh ingredients for my lunches into the office. I'd stock up on packages of romaine lettuce on Sundays, washing, drying, and bagging the veggies at home to bring in with me Monday morning. With a kitchenette and small fridge in my office, I was able to store the salad, along with any extra veggies and protein, for the week ahead. When midday would strike, I would put together my salad—yes, I make the salad!—and as people would come and go through my office, the size of the salad I made would reflect the people I would end up sharing it with.

It wasn't long before this little lunchtime salad turned into a social ritual. It didn't matter if it was only a few of us or a larger group; there was always someone stopping in for lunch. As I am a sharer by nature, it felt good to be able to break bread with whoever was joining me. The result of this ritual has been that lunchtime in my office feels like sitting down at the table with family. It's the sense that everyone is welcome, and with the common denominator of the love of a good meal, everyone is able to contribute to the conversation. Even the act of assembling the salad has become a team effort. The first one in around lunchtime knows to get that big bowl out and start chopping some lettuce. And while the little add-ons may vary—sometimes it's a few nice cuts of prosciutto; sometimes it's a can of tuna or chickpeas mixed in, and maybe some homemade treats on the side—when it comes time to dress the salad, I step in for the finishing touch!

This routine has been so organic from the start; it was a natural occurrence that just evolved and settled into an automatic part of the day. Anyone who's joined in on one of these lunches will tell you that it's a mixed bag of conversation. Just like a family at the dinner table, you've got energetic voices talking over one another, laughter as stories are shared, unexpected brainstorming sessions as some bring up issues for feedback, excitement as creative concepts and business strategies are born on the spot. A lot can happen when people feel included—and fed! And whether we've got fifteen minutes or an hour to really dig in, it's become a little ritual in the day that I can't imagine giving up. In fact, when any of my lunchtime "regulars" is off or I'm away from the office, it's our shared lunches and that sense of coming together that we all admit to missing the most.

This shared meal has translated to so much more than just a group lunch. It's a shared experience where those who are taking part on any given day can feel a sense of community. On some days, the focus is group input, as we've strategized how an agent can better support his clients through a tough sale. On other days, it's a story swap, as we get to know one another a little better through our personal narratives. The point is, it's an opportunity for us to sit down, enjoy a good meal, and just see where the conversation goes. And I have no doubt that for anyone who's ever taken part, this midday session has only further cemented the positive and inclusive environment I've always fostered in my offices.

But remember, just because you may already have a set of daily rituals in your day-to-day, it doesn't mean that they are all contributing to your life in a good way.

In the same way that our positive daily rituals can have a positive effect, our negative behaviors and rituals can quickly add up and drag us down. This is why it's so important not only to embrace change, and work to make room for new and fulfilling "little things" in our lives, but also to take an honest look at our lives right now and to see where we could benefit from scaling back or stopping certain rituals and routines altogether. By eliminating the things and behaviors that aren't serving us or our purpose, we are making room for better things that will.

Consciousness is key here. It is only when you take a step back, look around, and then look within that you can begin the real work. This is where my greatest strides in self-improvement have always begun—from within.

Technology icon Steve Jobs is a shining example of someone who learned how to embrace his daily routine and rituals and to take corrective action when necessary. "If today were the last day of my life, would I want to do what I'm about to do today? And whenever the answer has been 'no' for too many days in a row, I know I need to change something." Are you ready to follow his example?

ACTION ITEM #3: IDENTIFY THE DAILY RITUALS YOU ALREADY HAVE THAT SERVE YOUR INTENTIONS AND THOSE PARTS OF YOUR DAY THAT NEED TO CHANGE.

By taking inventory of your existing rituals and putting effort into the development of new ones, even the smallest positive shift in your daily routine will transform the hours that follow. You will feel more focused, energized, and *happier* than you were before because you'll be investing in yourself enough to see the power in everything you do.

HABIT 4

CHIP AWAY AT CHANGE

"You'll never change your life until you change something you do daily."

—John C. Maxwell

As we saw in the previous chapter, the little things matter, and that applies to change too. The secret to lasting change isn't always found in the big stuff. It isn't necessarily the product of sudden, major, life-altering adjustments. Real change is often the result of small, daily actions and behaviors, compounded over time. Looking at it another way, real change is the "take" for whatever you're willing to give.

While writing this book, as I considered the factors affecting daily change, I decided to survey some of my agents about their own positive and negative experiences with adopting new habits and implementing change, asking: "Have you ever tried to introduce a new habit into your routine? Were you able to do it the first time?" Here are a few of their replies:

"Yes, all the time! It takes a lot of hard work—for myself, several weeks. Some habits stick, and some don't."

"Yes, never give up; just alter the plan until it works!"

"Yes. I'm trying to do that now. I used to have a habit of exercising before breakfast, but last year, this rarely happened. I failed at this last week and so far, this week as well, but I'm even more determined to get this underway next week. To help me, I've created a mini vision board with photos of strong, healthy women who inspire me in this. I even splurged on some new exercise wear."

"I find some habits require many attempts before they stick. To be honest, sometimes I was successful, and sometimes I guess I just gave up, which makes me wonder if they might have stuck, had I only stuck with it?"

Most admitted to struggling with new habits, with some giving up after just a few unsuccessful attempts. Sound familiar? We're all human. We try; we fail; we try again—and the ones who ultimately succeed in implementing good habits, like good ideas, are the ones who keep at it.

Just ask Sir James Dyson, whose prototype for the best-selling Dyson vacuum failed a whopping 5,127 times before he was able to make his innovative design work. Talk about feeling the pain! But although the time, energy, and money he lost over that period of "failure" may have deterred him from forging on, you can bet his current net worth of $4.5 billion is proof positive that it was worth seeing it through.

When I was nineteen, I fell into bad habits that (literally) began to weigh me down. I had recently gotten married and moved out of my family home and into a new home, and life, with my then-husband. I went from the clearly defined structure and controls of living with my parents to the uncharted territory in my new role as a wife, trying to meet all the expectations that come with that. Somewhere along the way I started trying to make myself happy with daily indulgences in the form of food. In the beginning, it was slicing myself a little piece of pie or whatever after dinner, but it wasn't long before I tossed the idea of "portion control" out the window and just began diving in with a fork at whatever time of day the cravings struck. From salty to sweet, I was living life like a kid in a candy store! And then I discovered the McDonald's drive-through by our laundromat. I swear those big golden arches were calling to me. On laundry days, I would start the loads in the washer and then pop over next door for a Big Mac while I waited for the cycles to finish. One Big Mac turned into two. Two Big Macs suddenly became two combos with fries. And I'll be honest, I made sure I got two drinks each time—just to make it look like I was ordering for two! I can laugh now, but back then, the need to indulge and the inability to resist were huge red flags that I was craving something deeper than junk food.

As these daily indulgences morphed into habits—surprise, surprise—the weight began to pile on, and before I knew it, I'd gained thirty pounds. And at my height and usual weight bracket, thirty pounds was a big gain. You know how people sometimes say they have nothing to wear? Well, I had *nothing* to wear. Nothing fit! As I was a newlywed, people would feel inclined to ask if I was pregnant when they noticed the change in my appearance. I was mortified every time I had to look someone in the eye and say, sheepishly, "No, not pregnant." As my insecurity grew, I began to isolate myself, hiding out at home and feeling completely cut off from the world and from the person I now found unrecognizable in the mirror.

In the span of a year, I had slipped into such unhealthy habits that my whole life felt affected in one way or another. I knew things couldn't stay the way they were. I had to come to terms with my situation. The food wasn't the issue; I'd never had an unhealthy relationship with food before this point. The problem now seemed to be that I'd eat and eat and never really feel full. When I asked myself what was really going on, and what I was really craving, I realized that I was trying to fill a void in my new life that I had yet to face. My old routine had drastically changed once I got married, and I hadn't really taken the time to restructure my life. I'd never had to think about this before; life just was what it was. But now, the parameters of my world and my responsibilities had expanded, and I needed to be more conscious about my routine and choices.

What it came down to was developing self-awareness, day by day. First, I had to identify that I had a problem. I had to figure out why the problem existed. And then I needed to find a way to stop the bad habit and make a change. To do this, I focused on getting myself organized, planning ahead, and establishing some structure in my new life. I had to find a way to fill that void with purpose.

Making the change and taking back control over my eating habits (and new life) didn't happen overnight. Chipping away at this change daily, I set realistic goals for myself, including trying to take off three pounds at a time, which seemed to be a reasonable goal. It felt achievable—and I would do this by substituting healthy choices in place of unhealthy ones rather than by depriving or starving myself. It was about getting healthy—mind, body, and soul. Fad diets and dedicating my days to the gym were neither reasonable nor appealing to me. I love food, and I wasn't planning on giving up the good food, just the junk that wasn't doing anything for me! I knew that what I'd been putting into my body wasn't serving me. My system would get upset; my skin would react; my body was giving me all the signals, and from that point on, I was going to start paying attention.

Slowly, but steadily, I took back control over my eating habits, and my body thanked me for it. I felt my self-confidence build and my energy levels climb, and I began to recognize myself once again. Beyond the eventual—and healthy—weight loss, this experience in chipping away at change each day allowed me to see how setting clear, achievable goals could impact my life on a bigger scale. Change was always possible—if I was willing to put the work in on a consistent basis.

It's easy to develop unhealthy patterns in life, where we slide into bad habits and become overwhelmed by them before we even know what hit us. There's no shame in this; we're all human, and nobody is perfect. What matters is that we catch ourselves in this space and do the work to understand what triggered it and what we need to do to get ourselves out. Your missteps don't define you—what you do once you recognize them is what counts.

Unfortunately, too often when we think we need to make a change in our lives for the better and introduce new habits, it's rooted in some belief that we need to fix something that's "broken" in ourselves. We think we're unattractive, so we decide to lose weight. We hope to improve our status amongst our friends, so we buy things we can't afford. We take on more responsibility to prove to our families that we really can "do it all." And on and on it goes.

There is nothing wrong with addressing negative aspects of your life for positive change—but your whole life doesn't need to become a negative narrative. You don't need to live in a mental space of guilt and shame. And this is something I want you to begin your days with and carry with you into the remainder of this book: You are not broken. You are not "wrong" in some way for not having a perfectly refined set of good habits and rituals at this point in your life.

You are a capable, strong, and worthy person who is on the right track and who knows that chipping away at change will make things even better.

While self-improvement may include turning weaknesses into strengths, that's not the point we should focus on. Our daily efforts toward change and self-improvement should come from a place of consciousness, understanding, and self-forgiveness if we want to continuously work toward lasting and significant shifts in our lives. That's why it's important to approach change with a habitual, chip-away mentality. The other component to healthy, lasting change is curiosity, and your desire to read this book and gain some new knowledge is proof positive that you are exactly where you need to be—and I'm right here with you.

Are you ready to give it a try in your daily routine?

ACTION ITEM #4: IDENTIFY ANY WEAK SPOTS IN YOUR DAILY ROUTINE AND COME UP WITH SMALL STEPS TO FIX THEM.

Chipping away at change daily is all about taking small steps forward. Small, realistic, and sustainable steps forward. All while fine-tuning your ability for conscious behavior and self-awareness. And believe me; it's these small steps compounded over time that will amount to major, lasting changes in your life!

Ready for your next step? Let's do it!

HABIT 5

LIVE AUTHENTICALLY

"Authenticity is a collection of choices that we have to make every day. It's about the choice to show up and be real."

—Brené Brown

To be, or not to be—yourself, that is! The concept of authenticity can be a tricky one, especially when it comes to carrying it through every landscape of your daily life. Not to mention, all while being bombarded daily by filtered visuals of food, fun, and fantasy (and everything in between) in this new world of social media. With everything we're exposed to, and all the societal expectations we feel we need to live up to, it's not surprising so many of us lose sight of who we really are, at least at one time or another. So what does it mean to be authentic? How transparent and "real" can you be before you've left yourself too vulnerable? And how do you incorporate authenticity into your daily habits?

Let's start by returning to the idea of intention, because that's the foundation of so many things, including authenticity. And let's be mindful about this; we're not just talking about plans. When was the last time you approached a problem by asking yourself, *What is my* true *intention here?*

For example, when you're facing a conflict with your significant other at home, do you think your intention is just to resolve the specific matter and move on? Or should it be to uncover what's really happening beneath the surface of things, to really listen and hear what the other person is saying?

Similarly, when you're at work and faced with a task you're unsure of where to begin, do you proceed with an intention to simply complete the task? What would you find if you took the initiative and asked some questions—you know, dug a little deeper? You might discover a *true* intention of refining your time-management skills and becoming more comfortable asking for assistance from those around you.

When we approach our days without being attentive to our true intentions, we are engaging in every moment, every task, and every challenge with no real purpose or outcome in mind. This is such a waste! Why put in so much time and energy without a clear indication of what you're hoping to accomplish? What's the point?

Bestselling author and motivational speaker Wayne Dyer says that "our intention creates our reality." Understanding your true intention prompts you to live authentically; they go hand in hand, and you can't have one without the other. And, together, they build confidence.

Imagine this scenario: You've just started a new job, and your manager calls you in to see how things are going. Truthfully, you've been feeling a little out of place in your role, and although you knew your manager would want to touch base today, you haven't considered your *intention* for this meeting ahead of time. You also haven't dedicated any energy into asking yourself what it is that you had hoped to get out of this job in the first place, so you don't have a clear idea as to why this new job just doesn't feel like the right fit. So, you go into your meeting and answer questions on the spot, feeling obligated to speak positively of your experience so far, and because you're unsure of what is making you unhappy, you hesitate to speak up, or ask questions.

The result: You've spent not only *your* time and energy, but your manager's, too, engaging in a meeting without authenticity. And now you're back at your desk, frustrated and unhappy, as another day ticks by. If you'd taken authenticity and intention into consideration, you would have spent some time reflecting before the meeting. You might have figured out that the underlying issue with this new role relates to the fact that your daily tasks aren't challenging and fulfilling, as an example. If you'd asked yourself ahead of time what your intention for the upcoming meeting was, you may have realized that what you really want is to take on some additional responsibilities. A chance to prove what you can do! Then, aware of the issue and armed with a strategy, you would have gone into your meeting and asked if there were any upcoming projects you could help out with. You might have even established some actionable next steps with your manager. You would have left the meeting feeling good, hopeful, and excited for the change to come—and empowered by your own initiative in making it happen.

Which of those scenarios sounds more appealing?

Hopefully, the more authentic one sounds better to you. But how do you develop the *habit* of authenticity so that it feels natural as you go through your day? One place to start is regularly asking yourself three key questions:

What is my true intention here?

Am I being authentic?

Are my expectations realistic?

That third question is the logical next step to making sure your new habit actually works. You may have an intention, for example, of rising to the top of your company's management hierarchy within the year because you authentically believe you have great leadership skills. But if you just graduated from college and can only work part-time because you're a single parent, your time frame for achieving this might not be reality-based. Or maybe, on a personal level, your intention is to spend an hour a day with each of your kids, one on one. Your desire is 100 percent authentic. But it's not realistic—not yet, anyway—because of all the other demands on your time.

Habits can only be effective if they are achievable; if they're not, then we are setting ourselves up for failure after failure, and that's certainly not what our goals are here. They also only work when they're implemented with regularity, and this means taking the time to check in with ourselves throughout the day to make sure we're working on them. When we do, we'll find a heightened level of engagement, more consistent results, and an overall feeling of growing fulfillment with our lives. We'll operate from a place of self-awareness that will allow us to be truly present and in tune with our purpose at every moment of our daily 24.

When I first started as a manager, one of the new tasks I was responsible for was organizing and leading office meetings. As in many sales-related industries, the focus of meetings such as this came down to dollars and cents. In my previous experience as a sales rep, on the other side of things, the format was almost always the same. The focus and the feeling were always, Are the agents producing? How can we get more sales? How can we get this team to produce *more*?

I had the benefit of stepping into this role with the kind of perspective that told me this wasn't how I wanted to do things. This wasn't who I wanted to be as a manager, and even though the blueprint of expectation was laid out in front of me, I was going to do things differently. I believed that the success of a team had to be rooted in something more than just numbers. If I wanted to really show leadership and support this team, I needed to offer them tools and resources to educate and inspire them. I suggested we add more skill-building courses and event opportunities into the mix. I wanted to be part of a strong and motivated team, and I would start by ensuring we were really adding value to their experience in our office.

At the time, this just wasn't how things were done. And it didn't help that change was coming from a "woman in charge." Let's just say, I got met with as much pushback and skepticism as you might expect. But I knew that I was staying true to myself, and I felt confident in my strategy. My intentions were good; my experience was leading me; and I had the big picture in mind. It may not have been smooth sailing at first, but it worked.

It was never about trying to reinvent the wheel, or thinking I knew better than anyone else, but I understood that my success in this role would depend on my ability to trust my instincts and take risks when necessary.

Take your cue from noted research professor and bestselling author Brené Brown, who cautions anyone who thinks it's not worthwhile to tackle issues such as authenticity because there are other issues that seem more urgent: "you are sadly, sadly mistaken."

Authenticity is a critical part of my personal foundation. Without it as the baseline for everything I do throughout my day, whose life am I really living? What am I really working toward? What is the point, if there is no purpose behind what I do? Like you, I only get one life. Just the one. I don't want to waste it going through the motions to live up to someone else's ideals, reach for someone else's dreams, or satisfy the needs of everyone else. If I do, I'll run out of stamina and feel totally unfulfilled in my own needs.

But why is it so damn hard to connect with our own authenticity in this day and age, when self-expression and individuality are emphasized and valued more than ever? Why do so many of us remain disconnected from our true selves and purpose?

Many experts will tell you it all starts in childhood. Yep, that's right. Sometimes, in order to figure out why you're feeling so lost in the present, you have to travel way back into the past, into all those dusty memories, back to the last time you functioned out of pure self-interest, with zero concern for everyone and everything around you. Back then, when you were a lot smaller, your connection to your subconscious was a lot bigger. This was before the "grown-up" influence kicked in and you were steered toward societal norms and social expectations. Before that beautiful and carefree sense of self began to slowly fade.

Over the years, you developed a behavior-and-reward system, which influenced how you made decisions and what you were drawn to. Instead of simply going with your gut, you took outside opinions into consideration first, often thinking about what would bring the most joy to the people you looked up to and sought validation from, such as family members and authority figures. Eventually, you might have even stopped considering your own wants and needs altogether, as adulthood kicked in and your life stopped being "all about you."

That evolution into considering the needs and wants of others isn't all bad. It helped you become the person you are today and taught you about impulse control, responsibility, selflessness, and empathy—all good stuff! But with the good comes the bad. And here's the downside: It's over that time of personal growth that you developed a habit for tuning out that little voice inside. You started letting the opinions and needs of others chime in. You grew up, and that little voice inside faded, like a light bulb growing dimmer, and was left neglected somewhere in your subconscious.

I remember in my younger school days, it often felt like I was constantly being compared to my older sibling. My internal confidence—the curious, brave little kid inside—started to get drowned out by influences and opinions coming from all sides—school, church, and society's gender bias. As I internalized these comparisons, I began to feel like I wasn't good enough. I started to believe the external perception about my capabilities, and I allowed walls to be built up all around me, separating me from what society said I wasn't capable of. I remember my guidance counselor, of all people, discouraging my plans to further my schooling, trying instead to steer me toward a more "domestic" path, for which they felt I was better suited as a young woman. It was as if the world wanted me to stay "in my place," to just keep quiet and follow the herd. Everything around me seemed to encourage the idea of "going along to get along."

It took a lot of maturing for me to understand that these barriers put in place around me by other people, the ones that had left me feeling so unhappy, didn't have any real power unless I let them.

And I'll tell you—then and now—staying true to yourself is going to piss some people off along the way. Not everyone is out to embrace your authenticity, and you might end up ruffling a few feathers here and there. In my role as a leader, it takes some conscious navigating to be able to keep true to myself while also acting in the best interests of the people who rely on me and my business. Even as a parent, I've learned that while I want the best for my children (and now, as they've become parents, their children as well), I can only lead by example and hope that their own sense of authenticity steers them onto the course that's right for them. And that they always feel my support and encouragement along the way, because from experience, I can tell you, it's not easy when you're going against the grain.

As you can imagine, because I came from a traditional Italian family, it was a really "black sheep" move to get divorced—especially as a mother of three small children at the time. And while I knew then that I made my choices with the best intentions in mind, it didn't make the process any easier. But my gut was firm, and I stayed the course. I kept my head up as best I could, and I tried to manage that period of my life with grace and patience and understanding for even the cruelest interactions I had as a result. Was it an easy move? Of course not. But it was the right move.

Be true to yourself—it might mean disappointing a few people along the way, but it's not about them. If you're coming from a place of authenticity, then it's worth it.

Because, if you're not being true to yourself, you're going to feel it. Deep down, you'll know. And if you're in a place in your life that just doesn't feel right—whether it's personal, work-related, whatever it may be—then give yourself permission to make some changes. Your happiness matters, and if you're living in unhappiness for the sake of others, you're not doing anyone any favors. You're never "too stuck" to make a change. For God's sake, you're not a tree—if you're truly unhappy, make a move!

I'm reminded of the parable about the elephant and the rope. As the story goes, a man was passing a group of elephants one day and was puzzled to see that they were being held in place by just a small piece of rope tied to their front legs. There were no strong chains or barred cages to keep these large and powerful animals contained. He asked the animals' trainer why the elephants didn't try to break free, and the trainer explained that, when the elephants were very young and much, much smaller, this same bit of rope had been strong enough to hold them captive. As they grew, they never dared to try and escape because, in their minds, this rope would always be enough to keep them in place.

The limitations we impose on ourselves have only as much power as we give them. And just because something held us back once doesn't mean it will have that influence over us forever—unless we let it. By recognizing who we are and knowing that we are capable of anything we put our minds to, we can live our lives to the fullest. After all, nobody knows us better than we know ourselves. And in the same way that we need to make sure our intentions are realistic, we also need to check in with ourselves to make sure the limitations we perceive reflect reality as we incorporate authenticity into our daily habits. We need to practice self-awareness.

A TED Talk featuring *New York Times* bestselling author, psychologist, and researcher Tasha Eurich also comes to mind. The talk, which runs at just over seventeen minutes and has been viewed by over two million people (and growing), can be summed up in five words:

Ask *what* instead of *why.*

In her pursuit to broaden her understanding of self-awareness, Eurich and her team developed a study designed to sort the truly self-aware from those who simply *believed* they were self-aware, and what made the difference between the two groups of people came down to swapping out one word for another. Most people ask *why,* and when they do, they tend to lean toward the negative, placing a note of finality and dread on the answers that might be unearthed. *Why me? Why do I always act this way? Why doesn't he love me? Why didn't I get that promotion? Why did he/she lie? Why don't I fit in?* In asking *why,* we search for answers that might not be accessible, and we're left feeling defeated, frustrated, and sometimes a little too creative with the "alternative facts" we choose to grant ourselves when the answers don't satisfy us. Sometimes this means giving ourselves the answers that spare us from having to take any accountability. We don't like the answers presented, so we pass the blame on and wallow in self-victimization. However you frame it, it comes down to this: if you're not asking the right questions, you're never going to end up with answers that serve you.

On the other hand, asking *what* empowers us to change the narrative. *What could I have done differently to demonstrate how much I wanted that promotion? What steps can I take to make myself stand out for the next opportunity?* In asking *what,* we leave ourselves open to, and responsible for, answers that are both constructive and actionable.

One of the earliest *why* versus *what* moments for me was when I was twelve years old and prepubescent acne hit me like a house of bricks. All of a sudden, it seemed, my baby-smooth complexion was taken over by red spots and painful bumps. As a preteen girl coming from a family of immigrants and already often feeling like an outsider, I was devastated. This was one extra problem I did *not* need. On theme with my age, I spent a lot of time asking, *Why me?* Until I eventually realized no amount of whining and questioning would actually do anything to address the issue.

I needed to figure out *what* I could do about this problem. Determined to find a solution, I used the phone book to look up a local dermatologist and hopped on a bus to go to my appointment. I was advised to use a form of light treatment, coupled with a prescription for tetracycline. That was fine, but then the next question arose: *What* was I supposed to do about the fact that these treatments cost money and I had none? The answer was to get a job, so I started working part-time at a local snack bar. I was only paid a whopping ninety-five cents an hour, and I took every single shift offered to me, always eager to step in to cover for anyone else. Eventually, I had the money I needed.

My intention was to get rid of my acne. My authentic self stepped up to the plate and dealt with the issue rather than listening to those who said that my acne wasn't bad or that it was just part of growing up. My expectations to recover my blemish-free complexion were realistic—or at least it *felt* possible to my young self. And asking *what* rather than *why* steered me toward solving my problem. This experience further instilled in me the drive toward self-reliance and was a lesson in giving value to my own needs and feelings. At such a young age, it might have been easy to just write my problem off as vanity and suffer through it. But I was unhappy, and I felt that was worth addressing. No issue is too big or small to give your energy to if it means being true to yourself. And whenever I reflect on that younger version of myself, frustrated and determined to find a solution, I smile and feel a lot of pride for the stubborn kid who wouldn't let a few obstacles get in her way.

Most of us can think back on our younger selves and come up with at least one scenario in which we held our ground—or a time where we missed the chance to be true to ourselves that we wish we could do over. Whatever past moment comes to mind, whether it was a small triumph or you feel a tinge of regret—hold on to that feeling and use it as a daily trigger for authenticity. Whether the memory gives you an added boost of encouragement or serves to remind you of how far you've come and your worthiness of authenticity, use it to reinforce this daily habit.

So far, we've been addressing some of the inner obstacles to authenticity, but an external roadblock is often the reality of our current social climate. Think about it: in today's world, from advertisements to social media, we are being bombarded with completely unrealistic ideals.

From physical representations to emotional standards that are impossible to reach, there's no shortage of content out there designed to make us rethink who we truly are. Clouding our self-perceptions, we look at glossy representations of "perfection" with seemingly glamorous lifestyles, and when we look inward at our own lives, we are left feeling deflated and behind the pack. Everyone else seems to be "living the life," miles ahead, doing their thing, and looking great. We begin to doubt our own pace and direction. This leads to feeling derailed from our own core values and all the things that actually bring purpose and significance to our lives. And it sabotages our efforts to live true to ourselves.

Habitual authenticity demands that we learn to silence the noise around us long enough to look inward and listen to that muffled little voice buried deep within. We need to see all those filtered images and ideals, nagging self-doubts, and outside opinions as just irritating banging drums beating loudly around our subconscious selves and then tune it all out long enough to let our inner voices be heard.

"There's power in allowing yourself to be known and heard, in owning your unique story, in using your authentic voice. And there's grace in being willing to know and hear others."

—Michelle Obama

The benefits of authenticity are life-changing benefits and extend far and wide.

When you are authentic, you will find yourself better able to communicate, gain trust, make decisions, and accept challenges thrown your way. Your heightened sense of self will allow you to resolve internal conflict more readily, satisfying your instinctual gut and your mind. And you will be at peace with the realization that you can't do *everything*. Try as you might, and good as your intentions may be, no one can do it all. Even on my best day, when I've hit the marks I've set for myself and I'm in my groove, I am still just one component of the bigger picture that keeps my business and family wheels in motion.

One important caveat: being authentic doesn't mean that you don't need to maintain boundaries and prioritize your personal space and well-being. It also doesn't mean you need to spend your days being brutally honest for the sake of the whole truth or showing your cards to anyone who asks. But it does mean being mindful about transparency. Although, once upon a time, transparency in business may have been considered a weakness or sign of vulnerability, industry leaders today know better. In 2013, a study for the Edelman Trust Barometer unearthed some disturbing news showing that 82 percent of professionals didn't trust that their business leaders were being honest with them. Fortunately, transparency and trust building in the workplace are on the upswing, and this supports everybody's efforts to be authentic. I take transparency in the workplace very seriously and want everyone to know that I am being authentic in all my business relationships and transactions. Even in the literal sense! When someone steps into our main building, they'll note that my office isn't tucked away on the top floor—no, you can find me directly across from our administration desk on the main level. I'm present and in full view. It's transparency, implemented down to the literal definition with our open-concept office, which I designed with floor-to-ceiling glass doors. My own personal fishbowl, and I wouldn't have it any other way!

One other surprising and amazing benefit I've discovered about authenticity is that it's *contagious.* When you live authentically, you attract like-minded people into your orbit. When people look through my glass office walls and see what I'm doing, and how I'm being true to myself, they often do the same. And when it comes to a professional setting, having an environment of authenticity is more of an edge than you can imagine. Being true to myself has resulted in a reputation for transparency and honesty—and this is a huge added value when people are relying on you for guidance and direction. People know they can trust me, as a leader, for honest feedback, and in leading by example, I am reinforcing the kind of values and self-confidence I want my people to adopt in the workplace.

I'm in the habit of checking in with myself throughout the day, and whenever I find myself overwhelmed, I stop and assess. *Am I being authentic in this moment? Or am I just masking how I truly feel about what's happening around me? What is my intention from here?*

And don't just *ask* yourself these questions. *Listen* for the answers. I listen to my gut and let those instincts steer me. Every decision and move I make needs to feel right *to me.* Your decision-making process should never be rushed to the point where you can't take a quick pause and gauge how this feels to you. And if you are being pressured for answers, without the time to check in with yourself, you should pay attention to that as a red flag and ask *why.* This is how I do it, every day, with every new decision or opportunity presented to me—I check in with myself, and I listen to what my instincts are telling me. Trust yourself enough to be true to yourself.

Let's make this another new habit, starting with a first step tomorrow.

ACTION ITEM #5: TAKE NOTE OF YOUR ACTIONS AND DECISIONS THROUGHOUT THE DAY, ASSESSING WHETHER THEY REFLECT YOUR AUTHENTIC INTENTIONS, BELIEFS, VALUES, AND PERSONALITY.

I'm confident that, when you put this into practice, your day will run more smoothly. The people around you will work better. And you'll find yourself one day closer to achieving your ultimate goals. Don't waste another set of 24 by not being true to yourself. Trust me: there's no better feeling than knowing who you are and starting your day from there.

HABIT 6

BREAK IT DOWN

"Obstacles don't have to stop you. If you run into a wall, don't turn around and give up. Figure out how to climb it, go through it, or work around it."

—Michael Jordan

A few summers ago, during a family weekend in northern Ontario's "cottage country," I was heading out for a walk with my dog along the beach. My daughter decided to join me, with her dog in tow. You have to know, cottage time for me is sacred. It's these summer weekends away where I get to connect with my kids and grandkids—and can just take in the tranquility and beauty of the outdoors and the surrounding nature. It's become our family gathering place. And it's because of this need to disconnect, to "be present" and more conscious of the moment (minus needless interruptions), that my daughter and

I decided to leave our phones back at the cottage. We left for our walk armed with our water bottles and our energetic pups at our sides.

Off we went. The sand was soft and moist beneath our bare feet where the tide had crept up and receded back along the shore. It was midmorning, and most of our neighbors were either getting an early start out on the water or were still back at their cottages, preparing for the day. We'd been walking along for a little while, some distance from our own cottages, when my daughter's dog suddenly jolted with excitement and bolted up the beach, dashing between us. I was thrown off balance, forced into a spin, and landed awkwardly on my side. I felt the pressure on my hip as I fell—and then a white-hot, excruciating pain shooting through my side. I couldn't stand. I felt faint.

In a panic, my daughter immediately knew we needed help. Of all the times to have left our phones out of reach! Michelle ventured up the beach, trying to find someone with a phone. After a few unlucky tries, she finally found someone with a phone—a flip phone! But that would work! She rushed back to me as she dialed her husband, who was back at the cottage, while I wondered if, like me, he would see the unknown number and hesitate to pick up. Thankfully, he took the call and quickly made his way over to us on the beach. By that point, I wasn't sure how much longer I could stomach the pain before I'd pass out. My kids helped me back to the cottage, and I settled myself in to rest, hoping I'd only pulled a muscle or suffered an awkward sprain.

I went in for X-rays the next day and discovered my fall

had triggered a hairline fracture of the hip. For a few weeks at best, I would be significantly limited in my mobility. To have any chance at this injury healing on its own, I would need to be extremely cautious and patient with my recovery.

So there I was a few days later, back at home, resting up in my bedroom and feeling like a potted plant. I'm an active person. If I'm not sleeping, I'm almost always in motion—the idea of being stuck or immobile for even a short while was daunting. I knew I had to take this recovery seriously, not only for the sake of quick and optimal healing. The last thing I wanted was to push it and do more damage, so I would have to take this one step at a time. My first challenge? Making it from my bed to my bathroom on my own. I couldn't put weight on my affected side at all yet, and I was still far from healed enough to rely on the cane that they told me would be my new best friend when I started to regain mobility over the next several weeks. I needed a system so that I could brace myself fully but still afford myself the independence of going to the bathroom without a buddy system in place. I had an idea. I called for reinforcements. And chairs. Lots of chairs.

From my bed to the bathroom, I now had eight chairs lined up. It looked as though there was an empty conference happening in my room, but I didn't care. When my father came over for a visit and saw this scene, I had to assure him that no, I hadn't lost my mind! This chair train was my ticket to a little bit of independence—and getting to the bathroom on my own! I practiced until I had a system down, and from shuffling along the seat of each chair from the bed to the bathroom, I was soon (cautiously) bracing my way from point A to point B, holding on to the back of each chair, shifting my weight from one to the other and back again. Over the next few days, I'd establish a system for mastering the stairs too. Obviously, at this point, walking down them wasn't an option, so I extended my chair train into the hall and from there, taking my cues from babies just learning to do this for the first time, I slid down, from step to step, on my backside, grateful at every shuffle for the plush carpeted runner beneath me and the solid railing within reach.

Let me just add here, I'm by no means any kind of an expert in physio, nor did I think I had the perfect recovery plan in place. But I did know I wasn't going to just let myself be "stuck" or worse, constantly reliant on someone else for every little action. So just like I would naturally think my way through any problem to a solution, I mapped my way from point A to point B as best I could. The only difference being, this time, at least to start, that I mapped my route out with chairs!

I was initially told to expect upward of a few months in recovery. And while I was cautious at every mark of improvement, I was also eager to get back into my routines. Breaking every new obstacle and challenge down into physical steps each day, I was able to get rid of my chairs and my temporary cane, and even get back on my treadmill, all within six weeks. It wasn't a race, but I listened to my body and kept my focus on that final goal of a full physical recovery.

One other lesson learned here: make sure at least one person has a phone on them during beach walks! You know, just in case that friendly neighbor with the flip phone isn't around the next time the dogs decide to give chase.

Breaking down problems sometimes means having to bet on yourself and believing enough in your vision to trust the process with each step. And sometimes that means working from the ground up—literally.

Let me tell you another story, this one about how my head office on Yonge Street came to be. My vision was to someday build a new office on a piece of land near where I currently worked, and because my lease would eventually be up for renewal again, I knew there was no time like the present, especially given that my current office building was just barely accommodating our needs. I was piecemealing the space to make it work, and this wasn't sustainable for future growth. I also knew my rent would only continue to go up as time went on.

If I had my own building, I'd have more space for my business needs. And I'd have *control* over that space. I *knew* that nearby parcel was the future of my business. I knew it was time to take action. But that didn't mean it would be easy.

When the owner was ready to sell the land, I was able to negotiate a vendor take-back (VTB) mortgage for a period of three years. As the land was ready to be built on, obtaining the necessary rezoning would allow me to get financing from the bank, which I could then use to pay out the VTB. Obviously, getting the necessary approvals within the allotted time had me feeling the pressure. I was nervous, sure, but I felt confident it would all work out, and three years seemed like more than enough time. I figured the land was already situated on a commercial street and surrounded by commercial-use businesses and buildings, so it seemed a no-brainer that my project should be given the green light. The ball was in motion, and I felt like I was making progress toward my ultimate goal.

And then I hit a major roadblock, one that I could never have anticipated: opposition from the local community and local representatives. I was being looked at as the "big bad businessperson" coming to plow over green space and turn the community into a concrete jungle. Not the case! This stretch of Yonge Street was already bustling with development and growth; plazas, gas stations, and various other commercial businesses had already been built—all on a much bigger scale than the building I was trying to obtain zoning approval for. My intention was aligned with further contributing to the community's growth—not taking away from it. But as the three years threatened to come to an end, zoning approval just wasn't happening. And you know what they say: "When it rains, it pours."

The seller wanted his payout at the three-year anniversary, which was quickly approaching. At the same time, the lease at my current office building was expiring, and the landlord was clear: renew for another five years or move out.

By now, I had invested hundreds of thousands of dollars in planners, surveys, lawyers, site research, the works. I still believed in my vision for this land and the future of my business, and I also believed it had been worth every penny of investment. But now the walls seemed to be coming down around me, and I was being hit with ultimatums from the seller and my landlord. Talk about pressure—I was feeling it! I was at risk of losing the land *and* my business in one fell swoop. I no longer had the luxury of time. I needed to act fast. So I came up with a plan of action and broke it all down into steps I could take, one at a time.

My first step was to make a deal with the seller of the land. I was open and honest with him about the obstacles and issues I was facing with the process, and requested an extension—well, *begged* might be a better word here. I needed another year, and in exchange for his granting me the extension, I offered an additional deposit to be paid, in order to create some benefit for his end of things. It worked. It wasn't a cheap or ideal solution for me, but it got me the extra time I desperately needed.

The next step was to renew the lease with my current landlord. There was no way I could be left without an office, so there was no alternative here. Yes, it meant I was locked in for another five years, but I figured I could sublease it when I was ready to move into the new building. At the end of the day, this was the only way to keep my current business in place and undisrupted.

The third step was to get back on track with the zoning. I worked like hell to make it happen—meeting with city planners and giving assurances to the concerns from the opposition where I could—and, thankfully, the zoning *finally* went through. I got the plans for the building completed, and the shovel hit the ground as everything started to come together.

By the time the new building was up and occupied, the whole project wound up taking considerably longer than I'd envisioned. But my dream became a reality. What's that saying? "If you build it, they will come!"

The process from start to finish was anything but a straight line. Did I sometimes feel like I was in over my head? Damn right I did.

Was my plan perfect? No. It was time-consuming, stressful, and more costly than I could have imagined. But I believed then, as I do now, that sometimes you have to take a chance on yourself and your vision. This was an investment in my future—my business, my livelihood, and my family's financial well-being. It was worth every ounce of effort, every penny invested, and every step.

My ultimate goal and vision here were to not pay rent forever, and instead to redirect those funds into ownership, paying off my own mortgage instead of someone else's.

What are the "big things" in your life right now? From major life goals to work projects and personal deadlines, the list of important stuff taking up space in your mind is constantly multiplying, and not surprisingly, it might even overwhelm you to the point of disruption in your daily life. You may find that you need to start breaking these projects down into smaller pieces to manage them. Remember how we talked earlier about the importance of details? Sometimes they are the only way we can stay on track and not lose sight of the big picture.

Do you ever toss and turn at night, obsessing over every

unresolved task and issue? Do you worry about looming deadlines and external pressures? Do you ever panic about how you are going to get it all done?

All these to-dos and tasks can quickly become a towering mountain of problems, with a peak infuriatingly out of reach from wherever we stand, way down below at its base. The good news is that there is one common denominator, for addressing any big problem, that acts as the springboard from which we can tackle any and every overwhelming task on our list: the strategy of breaking it down.

Often, the thought of tackling something outside of our comfort zone can leave us feeling discouraged from the get-go. We respond by either putting the task on the back burner and leaving it to the last minute or by allowing it to consume us to the point of panic. Neither of these approaches is productive or healthy. Workplace productivity coach and speaker Melissa Gratias, PhD, says that breaking down tasks makes our goal more approachable and doable. It also "reduces our propensity to procrastinate or defer tasks." It builds enough confidence to get the ball rolling.

I want you to hear me on this: there is nothing in this world that you simply can't *just start.* And you start by taking whatever "big thing" you have gnawing at your brain and visualizing it in front of you. You back up and take in the whole picture, asking questions along the way. *What are the main components here? Is there another way to approach this?* By dissecting the task in your mind and working backward from your end goal to create steps, piece by piece, that will move you forward, you are able to set aside all those scary thoughts of *How will I ever finish this?*

And then you can get going with your first step of mapping out a plan. Instead of losing sleep and peace of mind, put your energy and effort into that visualization exercise and the process of breaking it down into small, actionable steps to get from point A to point B. You'll be amazed at how quickly and seamlessly you find yourself transitioning from step one to step two.

You might be tempted to skip this planning phase, but you'll thank yourself later if you invest the time in this process, and here's why. Life can present you with a lot of surprises. At any given point, our minds are filled to capacity with thoughts of family, work, and everything in between. An article by Nelson Cowan, referencing several studies on memory recall and storage, revealed that our working memory—the part of our brain where those bits of on-the-fly, temporary, everyday tasks live—is only able to successfully store three to five items at once. When you consider just how much you rely on this working memory each day as you transition from task to task, it's not difficult to see how a larger-scale project or challenge might take over and wreak havoc on your mental storage unit.

Approaching problems step by step works because we function best when we can channel our focus into one thing at a time. It doesn't mean we push everything else out of our mind entirely—that would be impossible, because we are continuously performing a mental shuffle of tasks, rotating our thoughts around and trying to tackle and address a never-ending assembly line of responsibilities as best we can. The problem is that when we attempt to juggle those things that our mind has categorized as the big stuff, we can almost instantly feel our system crash, and we struggle to envision ourselves on the other side of the task, issue, or whatever it is.

Down to even the most common of daily struggles, breaking a problem down to manageable steps has always worked for me. When my kids were in their teens, there was no such thing as "free time" for a single mom burning the candle at both ends. I'd always been someone who benefited from movement and exercise. It fueled me and worked wonders as a stress reliever. But amidst all the big changes in that period of time, from family to work, finding the time, space, and funds to join a gym just wasn't happening. The logistics alone of making my way to and from a gym at some point in my busy day were impossible to wrap my head around. It didn't work for me. But if I wanted to get back into active and healthy habits like daily exercise, what options did I have?

Well, I figured, *if I can't get to a gym, I'll bring the gym to me.* So okay—step one! I'd need a treadmill—just one solid machine would do it. My basement where we were living at the time would work as a makeshift home gym—all I needed was an empty spot to set up the machine, and a treadmill alone wouldn't take up that much space. Financially, factoring in the cost of gas, a gym membership, and babysitting if I planned to be out of the house while the kids were home, the price of the machine was worth it and made the most sense from every angle. Most importantly, I could get my workouts in on my time, without disrupting any other areas of my life.

In this situation, I'd been able to identify a need that was important to me, and, in eliminating the traditional-gym option that wouldn't work, I was able to map out the steps toward an option that did. I cleared out the space I needed for the machine in the basement. I set a little bit of money aside for a planned period of time in order to afford the treadmill I wanted. And after my new little home gym was finally set up, I carved out a pocket of time each morning that flowed with my family's daily routine and allowed me the space to get some movement in each day.

The result? Those small steps taken toward creating room for a positive daily habit in my life helped improve my physical and mental well-being, provided me with a little "self-care" time aligned with my needs, and instilled in my children the value of daily movement and prioritizing healthy living.

Nearly every "problem" or obstacle in your life can be made easier or more manageable by breaking it down into smaller, actionable steps. Look at the whole picture—what first step can you take forward? Don't worry about envisioning your every move right off the bat if that feels too overwhelming. Just that first move. From the little, "easy" daily hurdles to the big surprises that may come your way—get into the habit of taking a step back and pulling the problem apart. You don't need to have a solution or strategy right away. Maybe for the obstacle you have in mind, that's just not possible. But no matter what, you can always find a first step. And in my experience, the view to your next step becomes a helluva lot clearer from the vantage point of having taken that first one.

By breaking our projects down into smaller steps, we create a clear and actionable path toward the finish line that allows for satisfaction—and rekindling of motivation—at each checkpoint along the way.

These small steps also mean a smaller margin of error as you spot mistakes, tackle unforeseen issues, and successfully navigate your way toward that finish line.

Anything worth doing is worth doing right—ideally, the first time around—and this applies to everything we do throughout the day, not just big projects. And the more specific and clear we are, the better our chances of success. From the moment we wake up in the morning to when we turn in at the end of the night, we work best when we can clearly envision our next steps. There is so much going on in our lives beyond our control; why not simplify our lives each day wherever we can and make *breaking it down* a habit? Even something as basic as a messy house can go from daunting to doable with a simple shift in perspective and a strategy of small steps: making the beds, hanging up clothes that are lying around, and so on.

In time, you'll find that this step-by-step approach to projects and problems will add up to something much bigger than tedious chores; it will evoke a sense of joy and make it easier for you to manage the next list of things when they come up. They will help you "trim the fat," putting aside any time-wasting elements and negligible details that you might have otherwise dwelled on. You'll also find yourself more energized and excited to keep the momentum going, as small successes are known to breed confidence and spark effort. Finally, your checkpoints, upon completion of each step, will serve as cheerleaders and encourage you to keep going.

When I took the plunge to buy that piece of land for my future office building, there were no guarantees laid out in front of me. And even with a solid plan and identified steps to achieve my goals, unexpected things happened—as they always do! I was forced to adapt as I went along. But my end goal remained the same, no matter how many twists in the road and barriers were put in front of me. I had a vision, and I was committed to turning my vision into reality.

But of all the visions I had for myself in the early days of my career, nothing was more important to me than creating and maintaining the most stable and secure life for my children. And I'll tell you, when you're working your butt off to build something from the ground up *and* trying to be the best possible parent to your kids, finding your rhythm can be incredibly tricky.

When I first bought my brokerage, long before that land deal, I was overwhelmed by the thought of how I would go from where I was—a single mother of three, already working at max capacity—to where I wanted to be: secure, independent, and thriving. Sure, I felt intimidated at the road ahead, but rolling over wasn't an option.

So what did I do? You guessed it. I. Broke It. Down.

I stepped back and looked at the big picture—opening my own brokerage office—and then figured out the steps I'd need to take to make it happen. Step one was to develop the business skills I would need to perform my new broker responsibilities. Step two was to come up with a plan for my kids so that my new business venture didn't mean spending more time away from them. I had three teens at this point, and I knew this was a crucial time for them that would lay the foundation for the young adults they would soon become. They needed guidance, support, attention. And let's face it: although they were great kids, they needed to know I had my eye on them!

I kept thinking, *How can I lean into this new career opportunity, without "checking out" of my kids' lives?*

My new role required my time and energy, but my kids needed it more. I couldn't let either suffer, so I had to find a way to make both work. I chipped away at this thought—how could I do both? And then it occurred to me. There was only one first step here that would satisfy both demands on my time.

I decided to bring them into work with me. Step three was therefore to create job opportunities for them that would offer them a path toward personal growth in their own right but that would also benefit the business. Just as I had bought into this new venture, I needed my kids to buy into this new world *with me.* My two daughters learned the ropes at the front desk, while my son managed the cleaning. I was able to chase after my dream, and they learned discipline, humility, and ambition—values they couldn't have learned sitting at home waiting for me to finish out my workdays. This problem, which seemed insurmountable at first, turned out to be a blessing in disguise once I was able to break it down and look at it from another perspective.

Don't let the shock value of your problems scare you off. Life is scary, and your best days lie just beyond your comfort zone. Expect to be uncomfortable, anticipate the fear, and go for it anyway. Ready?

ACTION ITEM #6: VISUALIZE YOUR TASKS FOR THE DAY AND BREAK THEM DOWN INTO SMALL STEPS.

Think about a task or even a big project that's on your mind today. Whether it's developing a new product or reorganizing your closet, start by articulating what the overall plan or goal is and envisioning the end result. Then spend some time mapping out the steps you might take to get there. This might take more than one iteration, and more than one day, to get right. And that's okay. Just get started—right now, this moment.

You've got this!

HABIT 7

LEARN THE ART OF SAYING NO

"When you say yes to others, make sure you are not saying no to yourself."

—Paulo Coelho

Yep, you read that right the first time. In a motivational book amidst a sea of motivational books, this one is telling you to say *no*.

This might seem confusing for a few reasons. For one, the word *no* sounds negative right off the bat. Two, the idea of saying *no* seems completely counter to the idea of improving your daily life with opportunity-enhancing habits and behaviors. And three, shouting *"Yes!"* from the mountaintops is supposed to be the game-changing secret for success, right?

So what gives?

Listen closely, because this is something you're going to need to get on board with sooner than later if you hope to make serious changes to your daily life: It's okay to say *no*. More than that, it's necessary. *No* is a tool. *No* can be your edge.

_No_ can be your superpower.

But before I can help you see the power in *no*, let's talk a bit about why we say *yes*. It's easy. It pleases other people, which means they'll like us. It helps us meet our obligations and measure up to what others expect from us. And sometimes it gives us more control over our lives. You know that old saying "If you want something done right, you need to do it yourself"? This mentality plays a big role in why we say *yes* so often. We worry about others dropping the ball and, deep down, we enjoy the idea of being the ones to do it all. It's part of our ongoing drive toward perfection.

And sometimes we say *yes* because it seems to be our only option. When someone in need stands before you—whether it's a colleague, employee, friend, partner, or child—and asks you for something that no one else around can provide, you don't even consider an alternative to saying *yes*.

So, what's the most worrisome common denominator behind all of those reasons we say *yes*? None of them addresses *your* best interests. Sure, they might satisfy your need to be liked or might help you avoid guilt, but they aren't direct responses to your intentions or goals. They come from an external source.

Many years ago, I learned a lesson in saying *no* that I will never forget.

A fellow broker came to me, desperate. Eyes wide and pleading, he explained that his spouse was extremely ill. He needed to free himself up in order to spend time with her. My heart sank. I was gutted for this person, his partner, and his entire family—everyone who would be affected by the tragedy that I understood to be inevitable.

He needed to sell his company to free up capital during this difficult time and thought I could help. My heart said *yes* (even though my head was saying *no*). Conflicted in the moment, I asked for a little time to consider his request. But he pressed, saying that it was a time-sensitive matter. And I was the only one he felt he could trust with this.

I felt compelled to help. Who wouldn't? Sure, it was a big ask. And no, I wasn't being given much room to do my own due diligence—but this was life and death! Surely that trumped the usual protocol. And on top of that, he had a background in banking, which gave me some added assurances on the accuracy of the financials he presented me. So I agreed to buy his business.

Fast-forward to the close of the sale. Everything up to that point had gone quickly—too quickly—but I kept thinking the rush was founded on the best intentions under the worst conditions. The sale was official, and about as quickly as it takes ink to dry, the truth, as it usually does, came to light.

Listen; I can downplay it all I want in the name of diplomacy, but the fact of it is, I got played. The numbers I had been provided with didn't exactly add up once I had the forensic due diligence done, and the whole debacle was followed by years of courtrooms, lawyers, and a lot of wasted time, in addition to a huge financial lesson for me. Ouch.

And to be clear, the lesson here isn't to be selfish and lose sight of your empathy and desire to help others. Your empathy is not a weakness; it's an absolute strength. The lesson here is about being careful with *yes*; in my case, I should have listened to my gut before agreeing to help. If I had, I would have set aside my emotions, taken the time to weigh out what was being asked of me, and done the necessary due diligence. I would have started with a reply of *not yet* and then, after completing my work, would have firmly said *no*. And I would have been okay with that.

When's the last time you said *yes* to something? I'm willing to bet that at least a handful of recent "yes moments" just popped into your mind. Maybe a handful from today alone: miscellaneous work tasks, social invites, family requests, and even a few minutes spared to that pesky phone service representative who's finally worn you down with their latest special offer.

Now, when's the last time you said *no*?

Still thinking? I'll wait.

If you find it's not as easy to recall when you've said *no*, you're not alone. For a variety of reasons stemming from childhood upbringing to personal insecurities, most people struggle with *no*. The word alone has so much negative connotation associated with it. For women in business, even in today's day and age, saying *no* in the workplace is still perceived as being defiant and emotional, whereas men who say *no* are often seen as assertive and confident. In addition, most of us would rather just go with the flow and pile more responsibilities onto our plates than ruffle any feathers.

But this isn't sustainable, and research shows that the damage behind too much *yes* and not enough *no* can be both lasting and detrimental to your happiness.

The reality is that you simply cannot say *yes* to everything that's asked of you in a day. It may please others and lighten their load, but it deprives you of your own precious (and limited) time, which could be better spent pursuing your own goals and ticking things off your own lists.

There's also the likelihood that, in overcommitting to others, you are more likely to end up underdelivering across the board, feeling burned out, and resenting those you feel have taken advantage of you.

Of course, you can't control the constant stream of "can you just" and "would you mind" and "please, oh please" requests that head your way every day. But you *can* control how you respond to them. You can determine what is truly worthy of your time and your energy, and you can decide what your capacity is for each day's *yes* responses.

You can also shift your perspective about the word *no*. Think of it this way: every time you say *no*, you wedge open a little more room in your day to say *yes* to the things that really matter to *you* and that allow the freedom to live authentically. Sometimes saying "not right now" or "not yet," which I did only minimally in the case of the colleague trying to persuade me to buy his business, can also help alleviate the stress of saying *no* outright while you give yourself a little time to process. In my case, however, I should have taken more time to get to the right answer.

When you say *no* or *not right now,* you

- emphasize self-care instead of feeling *selfish*;
- let your inner guide steer the course instead of feeling *guilty*;
- value your instincts by being assertive instead of feeling *aggressive*.

Are you worried about how some of your relationships may suffer once you start being more selective about what you say *yes* to? Don't! In being more authentic and transparent about what you are—and aren't—willing to commit to, your honesty will act as a filter for any toxic, one-sided relationships and allow your healthy relationships to grow stronger and more mutually respectful.

Know your value. Your time is as precious as anyone else's, and you are fully entitled to protect it at all costs. If today were your last day, how much of these final 24 hours would you have truly lived for yourself and to your purpose?

Feeling a little nervous about jumping from *no* to *yes*? While there are times when you need to be prepared to break out an assertive *no*, you can also ease into this new habit with these clear-yet-kind phrases:

- Unfortunately, it's just not possible for me right now, but thank you for thinking of me.
- I appreciate the opportunity, but I'm just not able to fully commit to anything new at this time.
- That won't work for me, but let me get back to you if I can think of someone else who may be a good fit.
- Thank you, but I'm going to pass on this one!

Saying *no* doesn't have to come across as rude. Sometimes the delivery is what makes the difference—it's not always *what* you're saying, but *how* you're saying it. And remember: saying *no* doesn't make you a bad person. You are allowed to prioritize your own needs and to set boundaries. You are allowed to own your time.

Learning to implement new habits often means letting go of old, not-so-good habits. How many people in your life make a habit of asking you for favors because they know they can? Odds are that some of the people who continually reach out to you for help keep coming back because they know you will always say *yes* no matter what; that's the bad habit that needs to be squelched. Stop saying *yes* as an auto reflex or as a means to the path of least resistance.

From now on, make it a daily practice. Commit to saying *yes* only to the things that reflect your values and that you truly have the bandwidth for.

Don't make yourself the lowest person on the totem pole!

Start saying *yes* only when:

- it's productive;
- you've really thought it through;
- you know there is significant value there;
- it's good for your soul, not your "do-it-all" ego;
- it's truly worth it to *you*.

Trust me: saying *no* will open up a world of *yes* for you later!

ACTION ITEM #7: START A LOG TO KEEP TRACK OF HOW MANY TIMES YOU SAY *YES* AND HOW MANY TIMES YOU SAY NO THROUGHOUT THE DAY.

For each *yes*, ask yourself whether it met the guidelines outlined above. For each *no*, congratulate yourself because that means you are emphasizing self-care, validating your instincts, and/or learning to be assertive and not aggressive. Does the ratio of *yes* to *no* surprise you? I have a feeling it will!

HABIT 8

BE PRESENT

"Don't miss the moment . . . that is all we have."

—Arianna Huffington

On a scale of one to ten, how "present" are you in your daily life?

How much of your day can you say, with total confidence, that you are actively participating in, heart and soul, 100 percent? From morning to night, through all your personal interactions, meetings, and daily errands, and even the monotonous blurry bits in between, how much of your day are you mentally present for?

I ask because, and I know this is true for all of us, life just seems to get so busy. There's so much to do, and it gets to the point where our daily lives seem to center around how much we can get done and how many tasks we can complete. We wake up and hit the ground running, with tunnel vision taking over as we Zoom, text, and email from one situation to the next, all the while measuring our daily success by how much of our to-do lists we managed to check off. We do this; we do that. Quantity, quantity, quantity. Don't get me wrong; productivity is good—it's great, actually—but what about the *quality* of our days, the actual *experience* itself?

Let me ask you, if someone were to take a snapshot of you going about your day, captured in a single, candid moment out of your 24-hour stretch, what would that image look like? How would you appear, caught in the middle of your day? Would you be still, appearing engaged and focused—or would you be a blur, hastily moving on to the next thing?

Many of us would be rushing through the moment, eager to get to the next task. We might even look tense or on edge, as a million things course through our minds while we navigate every given moment. There are so many people counting on you, so many things at stake. You feel this weight, this pressure on your shoulders, and you carry that with you all day, right? And then the result, after all that rushing and effort, is a day half-lived, one you barely remember in any real detail.

Don't you want to feel that you're *fully* living life?

When we learn to be present, we master the ability to appreciate the "now," and this is when we thrive. We're in the moment, fully engaged. We take the wheel and steer the course from the driver's seat.

And that's where *you* should be, *consciously* navigating every curve and bend in the road. Only you can do this, but it requires taking yourself off that too-convenient "autopilot" setting first. You can master every good habit and behavior known to man, but if you cannot truly engage in every moment of your life, then none of it matters.

As someone with a very busy schedule, I know how tempting it is to just go with the flow. I remember the first time I read *The Power of Now* by Eckhart Tolle and something just clicked for me. "Realize . . . that the present moment is all you have," he writes. "Make the NOW the primary focus of your life."

As much as I love being busy and having a full schedule, I used to experience moments when I would be in the middle of one thing but already mentally moving into the next thing. I was physically there, but I wasn't mentally present. After learning to *habitually* and fully invest in my time and space, I've discovered there's a real element of fulfilment in doing this.

You take more away from life experiences, and you contribute more to the world around you, when you practice the art of being present.

A big part of being present has to do with your ability to focus, which is something that many people struggle with. In a world where the bills never stop, the to-do lists keep growing, and everyone around you always seems to need something, is it even possible to really tune it all out long enough to just *focus*?

Let me give you a visual: You're standing in front of

someone, having a conversation. At first, you're steady, focused, in the zone of this interaction. A few minutes go by, and then, out of nowhere, someone tosses you a small red rubber ball. You catch it, momentarily losing focus on the dialogue. *That's okay,* you tell yourself, *I just missed a moment. I can catch up.* Another minute or so ticks by, and another rubber ball is tossed your way, and then another, and another after that. Soon you find yourself lost in the conversation and giving automatic replies versus thoughtful responses as you frantically try to juggle all the little rubber balls in play, which represent all those ongoing thoughts rolling around in your head at any given moment.

Let's flip this around. Haven't you always been told, "Treat others as you'd like them to treat you"?

Consider this: You're chatting with a colleague about an important project at work. You've stumbled upon some road bumps and would like this person's feedback. Your colleague doesn't have his phone in hand, and he's turned toward you, giving out all the physical indicators that he is fully engaged in this space and this moment with you. And at the end of the conversation, you leave feeling validated and respected because someone made the effort to check into the moment and be present.

Even when we approach a situation with a genuine intention to focus and be present, we often find ourselves drifting off into our own thoughts after a few moments. Research studies reveal that the average adult's "selective sustained attention span," or *focused,* task-related attention, is between ten and twenty minutes, with the numbers steadily dipping lower each year as the individual ages. It seems our brains have been conditioned to distribute our focused attention in short bursts as they try to capture everything jumping up for attention.

But we have the power to change this pattern. In fact, focus as a tool for success has become such a hot topic that books have been written about it, seminars address it, and podcasts discuss it. There's no shortage of tricks and gadgets available, all promising to help you master your focus and as a result, master your life. I agree that, like anything else, we can choose to become more skilled at paying attention. We can retrain our brains to get back on track whenever we feel ourselves losing focus. But, in my experience, there is no quick fix for this. What it comes down to is good old-fashioned self-discipline around developing new habits and a genuine desire for change. You have to *want* to live in the moment so that you can indeed take full control of your life.

In the early 1990s, prior to becoming a brokerage manager, I was working at the sales level. It was a job that kept me on the go, as the many facets of my work had me mobile for much of the day. From door knocking to showing homes, I was always on the move. As far as playing to my strengths, this really worked for me! I loved the changing atmospheres and the chance to always be in motion. But there was a problem. I already had my eye on the role of manager. While I loved being in sales, the hours and stability of pay offered in the managerial framework were the better option when I factored in my children and their needs.

But this new position would mean a major shift in how I operated day to day. Instead of going from one appointment to the next, spending the majority of my time on the move in my car, I would need to become a fixed presence in the office. For someone like me, the thought of sitting still for hours on end was a nightmare. Even when I worked from the office, I was away from my desk constantly, walking the halls, comparing notes with other agents, pacing as I made my calls. . . . I just could not sit still.

I recognized that this was going to be a major issue as I moved from sales to management. I would be expected to show leadership and consistency for my agents and staff; they would expect me to be in my office, focused, and ready to support them whenever necessary. I knew what I needed to do, and the issue was beyond sitting still. What I was struggling with was focusing and remaining present in the moments when there wasn't some kind of action or momentum. If I was going to learn to anchor myself and be present in the moments where I would usually jump up and "find the action," then it would take a little conscious reprogramming.

I learned to make this a habit by starting small and committing to working from where I sat for thirty minutes, then forty-five, then an hour. I allowed for little breaks to get up so I could move around, do a lap around the office to network and make calls. After a few weeks of putting this into practice, I began to find a natural balance and rhythm.

I won't lie to you; it's not easy to habitually practice being present. It's probably one of the most challenging habits I propose in this entire book. And that's because, unlike waking up earlier, or preparing for your day in advance, *being present* is something that requires conscious effort *all day.*

When something is crucial, we put in the effort. And I've decided that, at least for me, being present is crucial. Life doesn't come with an auto-recording. You get one shot at every moment, and that's that. Of course, there are times when I feel overwhelmed and struggle to stay on track. But when that happens, I take a moment to check in with myself and realign my thoughts. I remind myself that this moment is the one I'm living in, and it deserves my full attention. It makes no difference what it is I'm doing specifically; everything and everyone in my life deserves my respect and presence of mind.

The "now" is all we truly have. And I've had to really train myself to be present in the moment. I look at each person and every interaction as an opportunity. One of my mottos is to listen twice as much as I speak. After all, we have two ears and one mouth, and if we use them accordingly, we can quickly see how this strategy of conscious and present interaction positively impacts our days.

Let's consider the benefits of being present in some of the typical environments of your day.

From a professional standpoint, the ability to zero in on the moment and be present is going to separate you from the herd. The common denominator across a variety of industries is *people*—they are the pillars of every great empire, the working parts of every well-oiled machine, and the pulse of every thriving workplace. Business leaders know firsthand that success is all about building relationships and solid teams through active engagement and genuine connections. And—you guessed it: this is rooted in *being present* when in the company of others.

I deal with so many people in my day-to-day, and I know it can be easy to lose concentration and get carried off onto other things as tasks and issues overlap. Getting distracted is normal unless you're a robot. The key is to *recognize* when you're being pulled from the moment and to make the effort to snap back to the present and recommit to the task at hand.

When you become adept at staying present, those who work with you will notice and appreciate it. They will respect your efforts to pay genuine attention and admire how you always seem to be "right there." You will become the example for what it means to be confident, detail oriented, and focused. And you'll find yourself catching things you might have otherwise missed.

Ultimately, being present in the moment at work is going to help you succeed not only in your day, but also in maintaining the traction you need to move closer to your long-term professional goals, not to mention also supporting a positive perception of you by others.

Staying present at work, all day long, demands a lot of energy, and unfortunately, it can contribute to the feeling of being bogged down by the time we get home—where we set the very worst versions of ourselves free. This isn't intentional, of course, but our brains function in a way that tells us to "turn on" as much as possible for the outside world and allows us to dim this setting once we get home, taking advantage of the comfort and stability this space tends to provide. In failing to be present at home, though, we are not only failing the people around us—the most important people in our lives—but we are also failing ourselves and potentially doing long-term damage to those relationships.

Regardless of environment, learning to masterfully, and habitually, take on each moment as it comes your way is going to be a game-changing confidence booster. You will discover just how much you enjoy being in control of your life and find a heightened sense of joy.

Relationships will blossom as the people around you will feel drawn to your newfound attentiveness and focus, and your family will feel supported and loved in your ability to prioritize moments with them. Even your time spent practicing self-care will be more effective.

So what does it mean, really, to *be present*? What does that look like, and how do you put it into practice? A few strategies that might help you:

- Establishing an awareness about when and where you tend to mentally check out. What time of day? Where are you? Whom are you with?
- Being prepared for your day, which includes consciously carving out enough time for each major task or appointment that lies ahead and leaving some wiggle room for the inevitable distractions.
- Physically demonstrating your commitment to others by making eye contact, leaning in toward the other person, and so on.

- Creating space in your mind for the moment, to allow yourself room to internalize, process, consider, and thoughtfully respond to whatever is presented to you.
- Staying on topic by committing to the subject matter at hand and giving that your full consideration before expanding onto other topics or ideas.
- Listening. That's right; *really listening* to what's going on.

It's not always easy. Myself, I empathize so much with young mothers in particular, who struggle with being present. I was always on the go. And while I found solutions to major obstacles in that time, there were plenty of family moments I know I missed out on. Was it a conscious choice to not always be present? Of course not. But sometimes, it's the subconscious sacrifice we make in the moment for the greater good down the line. And while I wish I could go back and experience every moment with my kids that I might have missed back then, it's such a blessing to me that I get a "second chance" in my role as a grandparent now. Anyone who can relate will tell you how rewarding it is—an opportunity to do it all over again, knowing now what you wish you'd known, or had the bandwidth for, then!

When we learn to practice tuning in, we truly hear the people around us, and they can see that we care about their day and what they have to say. When we respond thoughtfully, we are giving our time, wisdom, and energy to the people we love. As a parent, a partner, a sibling, or whatever role we find ourselves in, we can unlock all the joy and growth that come from truly connecting with the people who mean the most to us when we're actively present and we actively set the precedent for what it means to love and respect each other.

All it takes to start making this shift is a commitment to change for the better—a *daily* commitment to really engage with your life and all the amazing moments you've been subconsciously missing and checking out of without realizing it.

Have you ever noticed that the hardest part of a yoga class isn't the pretzel-like poses, or the long moments of holding good posture? It's the very end of the class, when the teacher tells you to lie down in Savasana, shut your eyes, and meditate. Gone are the teacher's voice, the labored breathing of those around you, the lights that bounce off the mirrors as you switch from warrior one to warrior two pose. You just lie there and breathe, and at first, your mind embraces the moment, physically exhausted and grateful for the pause. But then the thoughts start to trickle in, and then the floodgates open: *What will I make for dinner? Have they sent me that email I've been waiting for? How did Mom's medical test go? Did I remember to set the alarm at home?*

This is life. We start every moment with the best of intentions, but then just as quickly, life sneaks in and reminds us that there is no magical "off switch" for everything else we have going on. That's why mastering presence of mind, although it will never become an easy behavior per se, is so important, offering you both instant and long-term results, and why it is worth every ounce of effort, day in and day out.

ACTION ITEM #8: COMMIT TO BEING PRESENT FOR JUST ONE DAY BY OBSERVING WHEN AND WHERE YOU TEND TO LOSE FOCUS AND BY MAKING EYE CONTACT AND LISTENING CLOSELY WHEN WITH OTHERS (AND SETTING YOUR PHONE ASIDE).

Life happens whether we are tuned in to the present or not. And every experience in your day is a unique moment that you won't get back. It's a beautiful life; don't let it pass you by. Take a deep breath and look around you. The "now" is all we have. Check in to this moment and commit to being more present in your life!

HABIT 9

RECOGNIZE COMMUNICATION STYLES

"The way we communicate with others and with ourselves ultimately determines the quality of our lives."

—Tony Robbins

What is the universal quality we all look for in others—whether in a potential partner, an employee, or even just someone to walk us through our wireless setup remotely?

Solid communication skills. Communication, both verbal and nonverbal, is related to every human activity. And the ability to express ourselves clearly, effectively, and confidently is the characteristic that draws us in, consciously and subconsciously. It's what establishes trust and forms connection. How you communicate with others, from the very first interaction, will set the tone for the relationships you form and how other people view you.

It's also one of the few life skills that applies to every single area of your life. From closing that big deal at work to successful parenting at home and everything in between—right down to the little things you don't even think about each day. Your communication style plays a part in all of this; it's your signature for expression. That's why communication skills are key to your daily life. Forget the long-term gains here; just think about each set of 24 hours. How does your method of communication with colleagues, family members, and even with yourself affect your life, for better or worse?

For most of us, communication is a crucial part of the success of our day. Other daily habits, like waking up early, preparing for the day ahead, and being present, are also important tools that contribute to your success, but communication skills are what will truly make each day shine.

It's eye-opening to consider how many things fall apart and become missed opportunities, all due to a "silly miscommunication." But poor communication skills are far from silly; they can have a huge impact on your ability to achieve long-term goals and can ultimately be detrimental to your happiness if they become habitual. At the end of the day, solid communication skills go beyond just putting one word in front of the other.

Good communication involves a variety of skills, including effective use of nonverbal cues, appropriate pacing and close listening, careful word choice, and reading the room.

NONVERBAL CUES

Most people consider themselves to be visual learners, which means that most of us take our cues from what we observe with our eyes. While our audio receivers may work just fine, it doesn't mean much if our brains aren't syncing the words we hear with what we see. This means that, when speaking with others, it's not enough that we use the right words. We may not get our message across if our words don't match our body language and facial expressions.

Imagine someone standing in front of you, saying *yes* out loud while shaking their head *no*. How would you interpret this? Most people would say they'd put more importance on the physical cue indicating *no* because, as the saying goes, "Actions speak louder than words." Making sure your physical cues match up with your words will reinforce what you're saying, which in turn increases the likelihood that others will understand you, believe you, and commit to the interaction taking place.

Consider the last time you sat in on a successful meeting. Odds are, the person leading it was expressing important information—but more than that, they were also most likely making eye contact and demonstrating facial cues that corresponded to their message.

Does it surprise you to read that humans use twenty-one different facial expressions to represent their range of emotions? Effective communicators, like the motivational speakers who sell out stadiums and travel the world to share their wisdom, know this. Beyond the bright lights and amped-up musical cues, these expert speakers effectively communicate to, and connect with, any number of people at once through their enthusiastic gestures, animated facial expressions, and open body posture, which physically invites listeners into their space and makes them feel as if they're being let in on a secret, one-on-one. That's why these speakers go on tour and sell out event venues, even though their messages are also available through books and other media. There is no communication method more effective than first-person, face-to-face communication, especially when words and physical actions align. I've seen this firsthand as a spectator in the stands watching motivational giants like Tony Robbins.

And on the flip side, as a speaker, I know what it is to step out onto that stage in front of thousands of expectant faces looking up at you and having to anchor yourself in the moment and connect with your audience. It's not just the words coming out of your mouth—it's your body language, facial expressions, energy, and your presence. It's your delivery.

Whether I'm speaking onstage or even just running a routine training session at one of my offices, I'm conscious of my delivery, both verbal and nonverbal. I'm facing my audience, keeping my body language open and positive (no crossed arms or hands in pockets!). I like to be in motion, when possible, pacing to encompass the space from one end of the audience to the other, really making everyone feel included. I'm also making as much individual eye contact as I can, speaking loudly and clearly, enunciating my words, and making sure there's some serious personality to my voice. I want the message I'm trying to convey, whatever it might be, to really land! I want the people listening to know that I genuinely believe in what I'm saying and that it's not just talk. I've got some real information to share here! I'm also interactive, asking questions, encouraging feedback, and whenever possible, trying to get a laugh or two out of people. I want their ears open and their energy up! I want to bring real value to the moment, and I need people to feel my enthusiasm. After all, if I'm not excited about what I'm saying, how can I expect anyone else to be?

Nothing pumps me up more than celebrating the successes of our incredible sales reps and teams. Every year, we hold a gala to bring everyone together to put a spotlight on our people and acknowledge the incredible growth and achievements they've had over the past year. For the last while, because of the pandemic, we weren't able to do our usual in-person gala event, but in 2022, we got right back into it. And not surprisingly, this year, the energy and excitement were on another level. The thing I remember the most? That feeling of connection with everyone during my entrance and opening welcome onstage.

When we were planning the event, I knew I needed to

make this year's opener extra special. I wanted everyone to feel a collective excitement once they all made their way into the grand room. And I knew I had to make an entrance that would set the tone for what I hoped would be our best gala event yet. On the night of, as everyone settled into the main hall and found their tables and seats, the lights dimmed low, and the prerecorded audio started up. Then a countdown began on the big screens, my voice chiming in through a microphone, counting down with the crowd until "one." I'd chosen Black Eyed Peas' "I Gotta Feeling" for this moment, entering through the hall's main doors, dancing my way through the tables toward the stage. Everyone was on their feet, singing along, the lights overhead flashing in colors—the energy was electric, and exactly what I hoped for. Making my way up onstage, I joined my children and managers, and we danced out the rest of the song with the crowd. Facing them as the song closed out, I felt the collective energy I had hoped for. I wanted my energy and communication to reflect what I was feeling: this evening was all about celebrating *them,* after all! I stood at the end of the elongated runway that made part of the stage and spoke from the heart, expressing my gratitude for our being able to finally come together like this and my pride at having such an amazing team—there was no script here for this part of things. You could hear the excitement in my voice. This moment of communication was all about expressing, verbally and nonverbally, my genuine gratitude and joy for that moment.

After all, it wasn't too long ago that we weren't sure when—or if—events like that would ever be possible again.

In 2020, shared in-person experiences took a major hit as we were forced to put physical distance between us in order to mitigate risks of transmission during the pandemic. The massive spike in popularity of platforms like Zoom during this time is a testament to people's strong desire for that face-to-face connection. After a while, conference calls just weren't cutting it. People wanted the connection and feedback that nonverbal cues and visual indicators provided. Hearing someone agree with your idea on the phone is very different from seeing their physical reaction in real time via video. Are they smiling and nodding along, or do they look confused and concerned? And while these alternative methods of staying connected worked for the moment, I think it's fair to say that social distancing has shown us all just how powerful and irreplaceable physical presence truly is. Nothing can take the place of shared experiences, of really *being there* with one another, in real time, no screens or Wi-Fi required.

APPROPRIATE PACING AND CLOSE LISTENING

Research indicates that our brains are capable of retrieving up to 3,000 words per minute while thinking, but we are only able to listen to about 125 words per minute. That means we can think up and produce words at a significantly higher rate than we can process what we hear. This creates some real roadblocks in communication. One way to improve the chances for smooth communication is by being conscious of our pace in delivery.

Are you speaking so quickly that the message is getting lost? Take the time to really enunciate your words and express yourself in a calm and confident manner. This isn't to say you should operate in slow motion—you don't want to exhaust someone waiting for you to land on your point! But if they're struggling to keep up with your pace, odds are your message is going to get lost in translation.

Likewise, the speed at which we respond to others can also wind up being a communication roadblock to watch out for. Many of us are too quick to offer input and chime in instead of pausing long enough to really hear and consider what's being presented to us. When we do take a beat before speaking up, we allow ourselves time to really receive and interpret messages from others as well as create mental space to form a clear and concise reply, minimizing the risk of miscommunication going forward. After all, until I know what you are trying to say, how can I form my response? An old saying from the Greek philosopher Epictetus serves as a good reminder: "We have two ears and one mouth so that we can listen twice as much as we speak . . ." And here I thought I came up with that one!

CAREFUL WORD CHOICE

When we communicate with others, our word choice can make or break our ability to get our point across in the right way. Our thoughts and opinions are important, and they have tremendous value, but we need to be conscious of how we communicate them. Having a sensitivity for how our words might be interpreted on the other end of things means passing them through an internal filter before they exit through our mouths. Often, just being aware of our tone and use of words like *you*—which can sometimes feel accusatory on the receiving end—is a great start to practicing conscious communication.

For example:

"You really upset me with your comments the other day" can leave someone feeling singled out and attacked, often resulting in a combative response.

But if you phrase this from a place of accountability by eliminating the word *you*:

"I felt frustrated by the comments made the other day, and I wondered how we can resolve it so that we both feel like we've addressed the issue going forward."

This way, you've eliminated any space for defensive interpretation, taken accountability for your feelings, and left the door open for constructive next steps, all by being more conscious of your word choice.

READING THE ROOM

Successful communication is not one-size-fits-all, and you need to be able to "read the room" and adapt. This means finding the "baseline," noticing the nonverbal cues that others use, following the lead of others for pace of conversation, and paying attention to nuances in the dialogue that indicate when others feel heard and valued versus when they don't.

In my early days as a manager, trying to implement new strategies for support and resources for the sales reps, I came up against a lot of resistance from those who were used to doing things differently. Here I was, excited for the opportunity and armed with new ideas, and realizing, *Hey, no one is going to cut you any breaks here; you're just going to have to push forward and pay your dues.*

I went into a lot of meetings and had a lot of interactions at that time that taught me a great deal about constructive communication. Some people are going to come at you with fixed opinions and attitudes, and sometimes you're going to feel that as soon as they walk into the room. But other people's communication style isn't your problem; you're only responsible for your own reactions and your own narrative. It wasn't always easy, but I tried to see it from both sides. Maybe some people felt undermined by my approach, or skeptical of my leadership style—whatever the cause, I tried to keep the lines of communication open (and as constructive as I could) whenever possible. I've never had any interest in burning bridges for no reason. Odds are, the people you deal with today you'll see down the line in the future, and it's almost always easier to just find some common ground and keep it civil where you can.

In those challenging moments of communication, even if I felt myself getting frustrated, I resisted the temptation to get defensive. Instead, I'd hear them out. Let them speak their piece. I'd wait for my opportunity to reply, and I'd make sure I really tried to hear what they were saying—not just the words, but whatever they were actually trying to express. If it was totally unconstructive, I'd keep my head up and let it go. If there was some room or opportunity to turn the conversation around, or end on a more positive note, then I'd try to do that. The point is, if someone was looking to get a negative reaction out of me, I wasn't going to give them the satisfaction. And at the end of the day, my determinedness to keep it professional and be productive and respectful paid off. Go ahead and read the room—but remember, no one's in charge of writing your narrative other than you. So, whatever comes at you, be calm and in control of your words and you can't lose.

Adaptability isn't about being fake. Quite the opposite. Knowing how and when to adapt underscores your desire to be authentic while still being sensitive about creating the best possible outcome for everyone involved. In the same way we need to always be prepared to pivot when plans go awry, we also need to be aware, flexible, and willing to adjust our communication style based on what the current situation calls for. Adaptability can be extremely effective so long as purposeful communication remains at the heart of everything we do.

Reading the room, and knowing when and how to adjust, isn't necessarily an easy habit to adopt. Whether you're looking at this from a professional or personal viewpoint, this skill is one that takes time, effort, and—let's face it—a lot of trial and error. Most of us will never master the art of perfect communication, but one thing is for sure: when you work on how you communicate with the world, the world will work on its communication with you. So let's put this habit into practice.

ACTION ITEM #9: STUDY A KEY INTERACTION WITH SOMEONE TOMORROW, WHETHER AT WORK OR AT HOME, AND TAKE NOTE OF THE COMMUNICATION SKILLS IN PLAY.

Note the nonverbal cues that both you and the other person use. Listen to the pace, and note where it's too fast or slow. Catch yourself when you're too quick to jump in and speak. And ask yourself how, after reading the room, you might have adapted your communication style for better results.

HABIT 10

POWER UP!

"Energy is the key to creativity.
Energy is the key to life."

—William Shatner

How many times a day do you find yourself plugging your cell phone into a charger? How often does your remote seem to demand a fresh set of batteries? Even that clever Google Home device must be plugged in in order to come alive.

Nothing can keep going, and going, and going forever. Even the Energizer Bunny's battery runs out eventually, no matter what the commercial tells you! Everything on this planet requires some source of external power. The earth itself, home to billions of humans, cannot operate without the energy of the sun. Imagine, something so powerful and vast, and yet so fragile without its primary source of energy. Everything needs something greater than itself in order to keep going.

This is true, of course, for all living creatures, and as today's world seems to spin faster and faster, our society puts ever-increasing value on how we can generate or replenish our own energy. You can buy energy drinks formulated to increase your vitality. You can follow exercise routines that promise to get you going. You can listen to podcasts, absorb literature, and attend motivational seminars and energy-focused retreats. The energy business is booming!

But it seems that the more we try to refuel our energy source, the faster we think we need to run to keep up with the Joneses—or, in today's celebrity-obsessed world, the Kardashians and *Real Housewives*! Social media leads us to believe that there's such a thing as boundless energy and that it's the key to success. So we believe the hype and hold ourselves up against impossible standards. We believe that everyone else has clued in to some big secret to living their best lives, and that the right mantra or supplement or hot-yoga class or energy bar will be the magic pill to help us catch up to everyone else, only to feel surprised and disappointed when we inevitably burn out.

How come all those hours spent sweating my brains out in hot yoga haven't worked to keep my energy up? Why doesn't this energy bar have me bouncing off the walls? Is it possible I'm "immune" to the energy benefits of caffeine? What gives?

Many people are invigorated by diet and exercise, and

there's no doubt that they can make a *huge* difference when it comes to your energy levels and overall health. Although this is a good place to start when working to boost your daily physical energy supply, healthy food and workout regimens might not sound exciting or be the first thing that comes to mind when thinking about passion. I'm certainly not perfect when it comes to specific workout routines. But I know that, even if it means just dropping down onto a mat for a five-minute stretch, making movement part of my 24, every day, *does* energize me. And I'm passionate about anything that fuels me in a positive way!

And sure, the right supplements or a cup of your favorite java can help—I love my Nespresso (those George Clooney ads don't hurt, either!)—as well as engaging podcasts, inspirational literature, and motivational speaking events. There's really no shortage of options out there when it comes to energizing pick-me-ups. I've learned over time what works for me and what doesn't, so now I make sure to incorporate as many of these elements into my day-to-day as possible.

FINDING ENERGY FROM OUR PASSIONS

But these energy hacks can only do part of the job. When it comes to harnessing the kind of energy that's going to get you through your day successfully, there has to be something driving you at your core.

Your greatest energy source is your spiritual energy, and it's always within you.

I'm telling you: there's no energy boost like the one you get from working toward something greater than yourself. I'm talking about the big picture. That thing that propels you forward. The push that has you jumping out of bed each day. It sounds like a cliché, but here's the truth: when you're doing what you love, the energy *will* come. This isn't to say you love every aspect of your job, or role in life, but at the core, you know whether the life you've carved out for yourself just *feels right.* You know because you are passionate about what you're doing and genuinely invested in your role. And once you've found it, this core passion will be the thing that tides you over in those moments when you find yourself running low on your inner resources.

What speaks to you? What's your "mission" today? In life? What inspires you?

Between obligations you might be dreading but must do and other responsibilities that weigh on you, the reality of life is that it isn't always *fun.*

While it's easy to get energized for the things we look forward to, especially when we know they are stepping-stones toward our ultimate goals, it's the grunt work in between those exciting moments—those laborious tasks and challenging moments—that is a true test of our internal energy drivers. Take heart knowing, however, that when you are living a life of intention, with clear purpose and goals, all the effort and sacrifice of the journey will balance out. You'll feel yourself tap into energy reserves you didn't even realize you had, and you'll persevere with passion and determination when you can visualize what you're working toward and it's almost within reach.

So how, and where, can you find the passion that will habitually ignite your energy, especially when you're feeling drained? The first thing I recommend is stepping back and realigning with your intentions. You are the driver in every scenario of your day. And while you may not be able to anticipate the roadblocks and potholes to come, it's up to you to decide how you will navigate around them if and when they appear.

TAPPING INTO THE ENERGY OF OTHERS

You can also look *around* you for inspiration, strength, and energy. I've been fortunate to surround myself with like-minded people—individuals whose values and attitudes align with mine. But having these people in my orbit didn't happen by some happy accident. I consciously nurtured positive and enriching relationships, in both my personal and professional life, and have found tremendous gratification from having them in my circle. You are the sum of the energy and people you surround yourself with the most—the external influences that help shape your day and your life. Even if your chosen surroundings involve few other people, as was the case for many of us during the pandemic, you can draw energy from yourself, provided that your self-care practices are strong. Are you your own biggest critic or your greatest cheerleader?

Energy is contagious, especially at home. What you start out with at the beginning of each day, and what you bring home at the close of the day, will manifest itself within the walls of your space. This energy will bounce from room to room and continue to have an effect on you while also directly affecting the people you share your life with. No matter what kind of pressures and exhaustion I may be feeling from my work life, I make it a priority to try to bring the best of myself home to my family, treasuring my time with them, and regenerating my energy from the love and inspiration they give me.

CULTIVATING ENERGY OUT OF NEGATIVE EXPERIENCES

But it hasn't always been this way for me. Like anyone else, I've struggled and fallen into the traps of toxic energy along my journey. I had to learn the hard way that when we aren't conscious and protective of our energy, we leave ourselves open to some pretty scary stuff.

I was in my midthirties, married, and already a mother of three. For reasons that stemmed across the board for me at the time—relationship issues, career challenges, a need to assert my independence—I was not in a happy place. I had slowly allowed myself to fall in with some toxic people, and I was letting myself indulge in seemingly harmless "social behaviors" that began to spiral out into unhealthy habits and poor decision-making. I'll never forget the day that changed it all for me. I was home when a knock at my door signaled that one of these "toxic friends" had come calling. I remember standing at my door, listening as this fellow wife and mother told me her husband had gone fishing; she was bored at home; and she could use some company. Would I hop in for a ride around the corner with her to pick up some cigarettes and hang out for a bit?

I could tell she'd been drinking, one of those "social behaviors" that I'd noticed becoming a little more like a "habit" recently. Still, motivated by what I now recognize was a need for distraction, I made a split-second decision that could have changed my life forever. I hopped in the passenger side of her car, and off we went on this "quick errand." I remember vividly this friend laughing behind the wheel, and both of us feeling lighter in the moment with some company. And I can still see the gleam of a big silver truck parked just up ahead on the side of the road. The sound of laughter triggered an unease in my gut as I discovered—too late—that the person behind the wheel was more inebriated than I realized; then came the piercing screech of her car veering right into the parked truck that had caught my eye just a moment before. There was a loud crash, and the feeling of sharp impact and an overwhelming pressure surged through my body. She had driven the car into the truck, with *my* side receiving the bulk of the impact and ending up partially underneath the back end of the other vehicle.

I was the only one who sustained deep gashes that would eventually scar, nasty bruises, and painful breaks; the driver managed to walk away unscathed. And I'll tell you something: this experience, this "quick trip around the corner" that I almost didn't come back from, left me feeling angry at only one person: *myself.* As I began to physically heal from the accident, I started to dig into the events of that day. I was responsible for what happened to me because *I* opened the door to it. I literally opened the door to trouble. I knew better, didn't I? What could make a smart person do something as stupid as getting into a car with someone who'd been drinking? How did I get there?

I realized, in hindsight, that I'd actually "opened the door" to this long before that day. I'd begun living a double life, spending time socializing with people who were toxic in their own lives and had welcomed me into their little world. Somewhere along the way, I had lost myself. I had lost control and wound up spending time with people who were living in their misery while I drank the Kool-Aid.

In retrospect, I should never have gotten into that car—obviously! I am grateful that my then-friend walked away uninjured and that my own injuries healed over time. But the lesson of that day was burned into my brain: energy attracts similar energy—and my state of mind had led me to that place.

So what changed for me, after that experience? How did such a negative incident energize me? I took a look at my life—no filter, no sugarcoating the situation—and I forced myself to face my reality. The good, the bad, and the things that had triggered my need to find distraction with people who didn't actually align with my true values. I didn't want to end up miserable in my life—and I definitely didn't want to end up as a statistic as a result of more poor choices in the moment. From there, it took some time, but with each shift I needed to make, in all the areas of my life where I felt unhappy, I began to feel lighter and more invigorated. It wasn't the easy road to take in the short term, and eliminating distraction and temporary Band-Aids meant facing the hard stuff on a daily basis. But I was making strides toward a better life for myself and my kids, and nothing was more motivating than knowing that each step, no matter how hard, was taking me in a better direction.

And can I tell you? Since then, even on the gloomiest days of my life, when I've felt the most tired and down, my energy stays positive. It really does! Because I know that the moves I'm making and the things I'm giving my energy to are, in some way, aligned with my purpose. And this serves to refuel my energy supply.

AVOIDING ENERGY VAMPIRES

While I took full accountability for my choices that day, and the things that led me there, another major lesson learned from that experience was this: just as the right people will fuel you in positive and healthy ways, the *wrong* people and circumstances will drain you.

You want to beware of energy vampires. These are the people who swoop in with never-ending gossip, exhausting conversation, and negative energy. They aren't necessarily bad people, but the danger is that they are so caught up in other peoples' lives, judging and commiserating, usually to avoid addressing their own issues, that they manage to loop you into their misery cycle. These "Debbie Downers" will lure you into their toxic atmosphere—and if you're not careful, you'll wind up morphing into one of them. I'll be the first to admit that a teeny bit of juicy gossip here and there can be entertaining, but energy vampires can't seem to talk about anything else. Other people's struggles seem to fuel both their energy and their self-image by comparison. They are often unkind and cruel, and you don't need that type of energy in your orbit. Many of these draining personality types are able to find the negative in everything. They are "life victims," and it's everyone else who's wrong; nothing is ever their fault or their doing. If you can't completely shut them out, be sure to set boundaries and avoid engaging in their negative narratives. Just because they're spiraling out, you're not obligated to jump into that toxic tornado.

I'm reminded of a couple we once knew in our summer cottage community who lived on a nearby property. When it came to cottage "toys," they had them all: boats, Jet Skis, and all the high-end gadgets you can imagine. Their cottage was the ultimate summer retreat. It was "the spot"! And I remember one weekend in particular, when all the lake neighbors got together for a potluck-style event. This couple went above and beyond with amazing cuisine that they had catered just for the occasion. I thought to myself, *This is so cool! He's successful and generous, and he's really enjoying his time and space up here.* Who wouldn't enjoy a treat like that? It was fun, and we felt fortunate and appreciative of the generosity.

You wouldn't think generous neighbors like this would spark any negative vibes, right? Well, not everyone can see someone doing well without feeling pangs of jealousy, and unfortunately, as life has it, there will often be one person in the mix with something negative to say. I remember vividly, the following spring, one gossipy neighbor gleefully delivered some "big news." Apparently, our wealthy, generous neighbors had fallen on hard times. The grapevine whispered of financial troubles, which had supposedly led to divorce. None of this was anyone's business, and I couldn't help but feel extremely turned off, seeing how much joy this neighbor seemed to be taking in other people's misery. It was disturbing to see how someone who had only ever benefited from other people's kindness could not only find excitement in our neighbors' struggles but could also have so little shame about this excitement that they would feel compelled to pass on the news in this way. Talk about "cringe-worthy" moments? Well, listening to this neighbor spill the gossip on something that had nothing to do with them was one of those moments.

Moral of the story: don't waste precious time and energy engaging with energy vampires. None of what they're bringing to the table is going to benefit you. Besides, life is short. Be kind; wish others well; and worry about yourself. Mind your own business—because that's the only business that's yours.

MANAGING ENERGY AT HOME

In addition to energy vampires, another threat to your personal energy often comes from the space where you feel the least on guard—your home. And while many of the things that can drain us in this area of our lives are rooted in the best intentions and with love, we still need to be conscious of how they are affecting us, recognizing when they go beyond the normal and become damaging to our physical or mental health.

When Covid-19 came along, keeping our energy levels high became especially difficult for many people, in part because it was so hard to keep our home and work lives separate. The line between our two principal daily environments became blurred, which made it harder to find our grooves and to make the time, and space, to refuel.

We normally think of home as a safe space, where we can relax and recharge, but at the same time, family situations tend to demand the most energy. Home is also where we tend to be the most honest and raw versions of ourselves. The weight of things at home is different from any other arena of our lives because there is more at stake.

In 2020, our home landscapes changed, suddenly operating as our 24-7 environment—the home was now also our office, gym, classroom, daycare center, and even "date night" destination. For some people, their homes were no longer healthy and even became toxic. For others, staying home actually offered a chance to reconnect. We worked to bridge communication gaps and adjust our routines, bringing people into our personal lives over FaceTime and Zoom. Even celebrities like Ellen DeGeneres (such a fan!) stayed connected with their audiences by filming out of their living rooms with producers standing "socially distant" in the backyard!

Whether our home environments were affected positively or negatively during this experience, the universal, immediate effect was the draining of our personal energy stores, which then forced us to spend the next two years (and counting) trying to figure out a new, sustainable way of life.

Now, as the world is getting back on track, I really believe the lessons we learned during this time have helped us reimagine our home and family landscapes and have taught us how they can serve us versus deplete us. This means being extra conscious of how we exhaust our personal resources at home. The fact is, for most people, family is everything. And we are always going to aim to give 100 percent to our loved ones. But you can't give what you don't have, so if you're constantly burning the candle at both ends to keep everyone happy (I get it!), you're going to need to take a step back and assess. Are there responsibilities you're managing that could be shared amongst others at home? Are you overdoing it when really, you could be pulling back a little and giving yourself more of a break? At the heart of it, we give our families the most of ourselves out of love. But when you learn to set some healthy boundaries and create a more balanced landscape at home, you'll find it that much easier to actually *enjoy* the time at home—and especially, the time spent with your family.

FINDING YOUR OWN ENERGY-BOOSTING STRATEGIES

To reiterate, passion inspires energy, and family—as one of your greatest passions—may be where you get your fuel. But what if you haven't found the passion that energizes you? What can you depend on to recharge?

Everyone is on their own journey, and everyone is moving along at their own pace. *Recognizing* that you haven't tapped into your purpose yet is actually the first important step! From there, it's all about investing time and effort into unearthing what it is you want out of life.

What is it that makes you feel good? What makes you feel alive? What makes you nervous? What might prompt you to go outside of your comfort zone? What does success mean to you? Finding your passion—or multiple passions—can be a lifelong exercise, but that doesn't mean you need to wait forever to find your energy source. The process alone can be empowering. And of course, your *intention* can guide you, energize you, and keep you focused.

Meanwhile, there are plenty of other energy sources and strategies you can turn to. In a world where seemingly everything around you will drain your energy if you allow it to, you need to become your own power source. Rely on yourself for the strength and the ability to keep going. Be your biggest cheerleader, and keep set boundaries in place. And as we've said before, the little things matter, so it never hurts to have a couple of quick strategies to make energy boosting one of your daily habits.

One trick is to take a cold shower—seriously! By improving blood circulation, cold water helps to increase alertness. As a side benefit, it also reduces stress levels, improves your immune system, and even stimulates weight loss! I'm shivering just thinking about it—but when you consider all the benefits, it's worth adding even just a minute of cool-to-cold water into your daily shower routine!

Another trick that can be practiced daily is cultivating some personal rituals that help you recharge. This could be reading or reciting a favorite quote you saved on your phone for quick access, finding inspiration from visuals that resonate with you (this is where Pinterest boards really work well!), or listening to a motivational audio clip you've saved for when you need the reminder. It can be brief and simple; it doesn't need to be a full spa day. A song, a candle, anything that's familiar and that can stabilize you in the moment will help you refuel.

Preserving energy can be as important as boosting it, and my third trick involves just that. I have a saying at work: "Leave your baggage at the door before entering." And I also insist that, at home, we don't bring our work problems inside. When you get into a habit of bringing outside problems into your home or work life, you give yourself an excuse to lose focus and to let any negative energy interfere with the positive things going on. But when you adopt a habit of compartmentalizing your life, you can avoid bringing drama in where it doesn't belong. Setting boundaries can help you move from one environment to the next, minus any excess baggage. You can't run away from your problems, but you also shouldn't force yourself to carry the weight of every ongoing issue around with you all day. Handle what you need to in its appropriate space and time, without giving it access to every other corner of your life. Protect your sanity, your space, and your energy reserves with healthy boundaries and an awareness of how other people affect you.

Finally, stay positive, even in the face of failures—and always maintain the ability to laugh at yourself! You have everything you need within you, and so far, you have already survived 100 percent of your worst days. You've got this!

ACTION ITEM #10: PRACTICE RECHARGING FROM WITHIN.

Identify the people in your life who invigorate you. Take inventory of where energy drains lurk in your work and home environments. And develop a simple, daily personal ritual that can recharge you instantly without a significant time or financial investment.

HABIT 11

MANAGE YOUR SOCIAL MEDIA PRESENCE

"If you are on social media, and you are not learning, not laughing, not being inspired, or not networking, then you are using it wrong."

—Germany Kent

I recently took a nearly one-year break from social media. I just unplugged from my personal page and took a pause. We were all still in the middle of the pandemic, and social media platforms were seeing record-breaking numbers in engagement. This was when I was dealing with a health scare amongst other things, and to be honest, social media just started to feel like a lot of effort. It was taking me in an inauthentic direction just to keep it going on a consistent basis, and I really didn't want to put things "out there" unless it was coming from a genuine place.

So I took a break. And you know what? I survived!

The break gave me the time and space I needed to reevaluate what I wanted my space in this social media world to be. Until I figured out what that was, I was better off giving it a rest.

My absence didn't go unnoticed, and it wasn't long before people started "checking in." I'll admit; it was flattering to know that people noticed when I logged off from the platforms. My online community was still a network made up of many people who were part of my personal and professional "real life," so I knew there might be some curiosity. I definitely appreciated it when people said they missed my posts and funny little videos, but I still needed to figure out how relevant social media was to me.

At that time, there were roughly 3.5 billion active social media users in the world. *Billion*—with a *b*. This is equal to nearly half of the world's population. Seriously. Half of the living, breathing humans on this planet were online. It's mind-blowing to think how far we've come in just twenty-odd years, when the first social media platform, SixDegrees, was launched. (Does anyone out there remember it?) The very concept of online social networking was completely foreign to most of us, and in just three short decades, we've now come together on a global scale to share our worlds with one another online.

This idea of connection from a distance has totally

changed the game in terms of social interaction. And while I can admit that I was initially hesitant about what role social media could (or should) play in my life, I have to say that I've really come around! The way I see it, the power of social media lies in its users. The technology itself is close to perfect; the platform is free, and the reach is limitless. Come one, come all, right? Whether it succeeds or fails lies with the human variable. It's up to us.

And with half the world watching, there are some major risks and pitfalls to avoid in social networking, and attending to these as part of your daily practice is paramount to a successful relationship with the online world.

One caveat is getting too comfortable with your online presence, because the temptation is to overshare. As with any arena in life, setting clear boundaries with your relationships is healthy—and necessary—for your self-care and sanity. This goes for your online community too! Treating your social media platforms as a no-filter zone isn't being authentic; it's being irresponsible. Remember, the internet is forever, so before you post something you'll regret—from angry tweets that might offend someone to sloppy images from a night out with close friends—take a minute to think it over. If you still think the message might be worth sharing (with 3.5 billion people), save it in your drafts and sleep on it. Better safe than sorry!

Knowing your audience is also a must. In real life (or "IRL" in social media lingo), how you present yourself is generally consistent, but it varies a little depending on your environment. You wouldn't let your hair down at work the same way you do at home, and your persona with colleagues differs from the way you behave amongst close friends. This isn't being fake; it's just good common sense. You're still you, after all. You just *know your audience* and act accordingly.

It's different on social media platforms like Instagram, where the risk is *unintentional misrepresentation.* You might be willing and eager to share some great content, but because you don't always have the space for context, viewers might not be able to tell if you're serious or sarcastic. They might see something as controversial that you didn't view that way. They may take offense to a message you didn't even realize was coming across. The list of potential misfires goes on. It's not like sharing a full story with people sitting in front of you. On platforms like Instagram, it boils down to an image presented to the world with a few words and a couple hashtags to go along with it. And then poof! It's out there for people to internalize, interpret, and judge however they choose.

Another important thing to think about is how your social media life fits into your daily routine. Call me a buzzkill, but I've seen a lot of people around me, both personally and professionally, fail on social media—or fail in other aspects of life because of it. As of 2021, American users between eighteen and thirty-four years of age ran an average of eight social media accounts, and these numbers have continued to grow. With no shortage of free and easily accessible social media platforms, the risk is that you can easily become distracted from other things that matter in your day.

Just think about it: How many times have you woken up,

picked up your phone before getting out of bed, and fallen down the rabbit hole of Instagram feed scrolling? Before you know it, an hour (or more!) has gone by, and you've got nothing to show for all that time invested other than a few shares of the latest viral video, some funny memes, and an update on the lives of everyone who's posted that morning. Not exactly groundbreaking stuff here. And while there's no harm in taking part in the fun of social media, you need to be careful not to lose track of real life in the process.

Distraction shows up in another way too. When we spend so much time looking at the glossy, filtered lives of others (as they appear to be, anyway), we are distracted from reality and what really matters. Don't get me wrong; some of those filters can be fun to play around with—I can admit that I used to like the superflattering "beauty cam" option. But don't waste your day living in that space, obsessing over "perfect" faces and curated posts; out here in the real world is where the action is!

In a 2021 segment on CNN, celebrated news anchor Anderson Cooper spoke candidly about his views on social media, especially in regard to its effects on young people, as well as his own experiences with social outlets. He admitted to enjoying platforms like Instagram for the ability to interact with friends and scroll through pages that catered to his specific interests, but the downside was the aftereffects, which often left him feeling worse than when he logged on.

There's no doubting the entertainment value and obvious benefits of social media, but overexposure has taken a toll on many people's ability to keep a clear divider between fantasy and reality. Not to mention the natural impulse to compare our own lives to those we see others living through their online profiles.

Remember: you're not in competition with the people you see online, and all those curated images do not reflect the full scope of anyone's life.

So how *should* you carve out your social media space? That all depends on whether your profiles will be private, reserved for close friends and family, or public and available for the world to see without restrictions. Another consideration is whether you're looking to create a professional platform and build your brand online, or if this is a hobby space, designed to reach people with common interests and to nurture your creative side. Being able to answer these questions will bring you closer to defining your goals with social networking and allow you to make the most of your daily experience with it.

Your intentions and the amount of time you devote to managing social media will determine what you get out of it.

In the business world, the fact is that you can't avoid the social media machine. It's a powerhouse of epic proportions, and it plays a major role in nearly every professional industry in existence. Simply put, if you want to thrive in your work, you're going to have to incorporate the online world into your daily routine. It all starts with *intention*, like all the other habits in your 24. You need to know what you hope to get out of the social-sharing experience before you can decide what to put into it.

In 2019 alone, $90 billion was spent on social-network advertising. Currently, roughly five hundred million Facebook users view eight billion videos every day, and over ninety-five million photos are shared each day on Instagram. There's a major potential client pool out there, growing by the minute, and you have a direct line to them without restrictions of distance or time. If your intention is to target messages to an audience that's already curious about your product or message, you can manage your content accordingly. And if your intention is to reach a lot of new people affordably, social media gives you plenty of options for that too.

Another intention that drives a lot of social media activity is the desire to get quick feedback about your audience and your industry. Nearly all platforms offer insights that allow users to see *how* their content is doing, *whom* it's reaching, and *when* and *where* it's been the most effective. These insights also help you stay on top of industry trends and even compare your media strategies to those of your competitors, which can level a playing field amongst users of various sizes and with various resources.

But regardless of your intention, one of the best things that social media has to offer is that it allows you to show how original you are and to use your own style and creativity to your advantage. And your biggest advantage here is *you*. You may be promoting the same business or trying to grow followers for a popular interest amongst a sea of similar accounts—but you are an original. Defining what you hope to get out of the experience will allow you to step into this social network with clear boundaries and goals—leaving you free to get creative.

I have agents tapping into new client pools by participating in fun and trending Tik Tok videos and others who are going viral from simple, catchy Instagram Reels. It's incredible to see how a simple but innovative "house tour" video, using just the right pace and visuals and audio, can go viral and capture millions of views.

I know the power of this social media machine because I'm seeing it play out in new ways every day, and I use it as my space to inspire. I get real with my followers and offer glimpses into my daily life that are relevant to my cause. Relying on positivity, motivation, and authenticity, I let others know what works for me and what gets me excited about life. In turn, I get to meet and hear from people all over the world who share my energy.

But how did I turn this into a habit? The truth is that I post when I'm feeling it, and I think my genuine enthusiasm in the moments and things I choose to share comes across best that way. But the keys to forming habits are structure and consistency, right? So, while I struggle not to post unless something really feels "right," I know this platform is a tool that needs to be managed in a consistent and fluid way. I am fortunate to have a social media team assist me with this internal conflict. They are in charge of engagement and scheduling, and my habit here has become checking in on my social media once a day and retrieving updates from my team. Not every habit requires major compromise; sometimes it just takes finding a different way to arrive at the same result.

ACTION ITEM #11: TAKE A LOOK AT YOUR SOCIAL MEDIA FOOTPRINT, MAKING CONSCIOUS CHOICES ABOUT THE ROLE IT PLAYS IN YOUR LIFE AND SETTING CLEAR LIMITS ON THE TIME YOU'RE WILLING TO GIVE TO IT EACH DAY.

Does it represent your personal and/or professional intentions? Are you on the right platforms? Are you careful with your engagement approach? Remember: there are 3.5 billion+ people logged in . . . and waiting for you! Don't deprive yourself of the interaction and entertainment if that's what interests you—but set some boundaries to keep yourself accountable for how much of your time you're giving to this online world.

HABIT 12

TAKE INVENTORY

"You cannot have a meaningful life without self-reflection."

—Oprah Winfrey

One of the most powerful habits, and tools for growth, that you can implement is self-reflection, which I find especially helpful as the day draws near the end. So much happens in a single day, and it can feel like it passes us in a blur. You may already find yourself asking, *How is it already six o'clock? Where did the day go?*

My days are chaotic—but not in a bad way. There's just so much going on that, some days, it feels as though I blink and it's already creeping up on six o'clock. (Not that any particular hour means much to me—I leave the office when I'm done for the day, not when the clock tells me to!) It can be tempting to just shrug and say, *Oh well, another day's flown by somehow.* But that's not how we grow, is it?

Growth comes from self-awareness, and taking personal inventory each day is all about reflection, accountability, and actionable next steps. Yes, it can definitely feel like *more* work—hence the appeal in blowing it off. You're tired. You're fried! You're eager to kick back and relax. The last thing you feel like doing is hitting "replay" on the day's events. I get it. You're human—you are not a robot!

But here's the thing, folks: without looking at, and even measuring, your progress each day, you can't know if you're headed in the right direction or not. Taking inventory is also a way to clear your slate for the next day. Why keep those bricks in the bag? Good or bad, there's no point carrying today into tomorrow—so let's get on with it!

Contrary to what you might think, self-reflection, or taking inventory of the day, isn't a tedious task of running through the day's events and making sure you completed every little thing on your schedule. Wrong, wrong, wrong. This couldn't be less true of what *effective* daily reflection is all about.

The *Cambridge Dictionary* defines self-reflection as "the activity of thinking about your own feelings and behavior, and the reasons that may lie behind them." That's closer to what I'm talking about, but Dr. Geil Browning, a big believer in the power of self-reflection, goes a little further. She is the founder and CEO of Emergenetics, a company that uses behavioral profiles based on genetics and life experiences to help individuals gain insight into the *why* behind their thought patterns and behaviors. For her, self-reflection is "a deeper form of learning that allows us to retain every aspect of any experience." She describes how by practicing self-reflection you are truly able to see each life experience and determine why it happened, its impact, and whether you'd like it to occur again rather than just recalling the experience. It helps us to zero in on what is truly important to us.

Taking inventory, then, is less about the events that happened and more about the driving forces behind them, and the impact they have on you after the fact—both good and not so good.

Think about all the decisions and actions you make in a single day. Now imagine having some real insight as to what led you to make those choices. Understanding your own motivations, and recognizing where you might be slipping away from your intentions and goals, is key to staying on track each day. Committing to living your purpose and working toward your greatest potential also helps you hold yourself accountable and recognize your own missteps and triggers.

But accountability doesn't have to be about shaming yourself for the low points of the day or writing them off as failures. You can let go of all that guilt and simply open yourself up to learn from your mistakes because they're just part of the process. This is all about growth!

When is the best time to practice self-reflection? Although you can do it at any time, I find that it's most useful toward the end of my day—but it's not the very last thing I do.

Think about it. Have you ever woken up from a bizarre

dream and been amazed at just how much detail you could remember? The characters, the settings, even the bizarre themes—all of it still vivid in your mind. Now, have you ever tried to recall that same dream a few hours later? Not so easy.

The same goes for your day's events, as the details of your daily memories will begin fading the longer you wait to reflect on them. According to German psychologist Hermann Ebbinghaus, who created the Forgetting Curve theory, our brains will forget an average of up to 70 percent of new information within 24 hours. This is why you'll find so many successful people choose to *start* the final chapter of their day with self-reflection, before those memories can get fuzzy or are forgotten entirely. They don't wait until the end of the day.

While taking the time for self-reflection will require some effort if you're new to it, this won't always be the case. Like all the daily habits and behaviors we've discussed, this is another one of those things that, with repetition, will eventually become an autopilot behavior—an automatic gear your mind will shift into at a specific point each day as the habit takes over and you ease into a reflective state.

So how exactly do you take personal inventory? The specifics are up to you, but the key is making sure you are looking through the right lens. Remember that the goal here is not to simply hit "replay" on the day's events. You've already lived it once, and that's enough, right? The goal should be to take a glance at your day to isolate any pockets where achievements were met or mistakes were made. In other words, isolate the highs and lows and go from there. You might keep a physical journal, noting down some of your thoughts or actionable steps you'd like to take going into the next day, or it may just be a mental plan you carve out for yourself in thought—however you choose to carry and implement your next steps.

Need some help to get the ball rolling? Try asking yourself the following:

What were the high/low points of my day?

I have gratitude for the events of the day, but do I feel I could have done better in some area?

Do I feel closer to my goals? Did my short-term decision-making process today feed into my long-term goals? If not, why not?

What did I do (or not do) today that I would like to do differently tomorrow?

Asking yourself these questions is the easy part. Coming up with the honest answers can be a little more difficult. But it's worth it! It is always worth the time and energy to dig deeper and be honest with yourself to identify mistakes, problematic triggers, and unproductive patterns so that you can make different choices in the future. And the reason you'll appreciate practicing this every day is that a single day can change everything.

You never know what hidden lesson or key moment from a 24-hour span might surface to present an opportunity for growth and catapult you into your greatest life.

An added side benefit of this practice is that it helps us hold on to, or reclaim, control. In 2020, our lives were flipped upside down to accommodate a rapidly changing world, mostly without our input or control. Let's be honest; that didn't feel great. No one likes to give up the reins, and there's not a lot of comfort in knowing that things can change on a dime from day to day. But we cannot let things beyond our control consume us. Times of struggle and crisis will come and go, and learning how to recognize the impact that external factors have on us, on any given day, is what will empower us to move forward. Why not take full advantage of the things that *are* in our control? Why not shift your perspective and see this as the ultimate moment for personal growth?

Your life matters. Your time matters. What you do each and every hour matters, including the lessons you take from one day to the next, and self-reflection is the tool we use to counterbalance loss of control. It gives us the chance to time-travel into the recent past, pinpoint the holes in our days, replay the moments we wish could have been different, and even celebrate any daily achievements all over again. Through this process, we essentially reclaim the day, and while we can't change anything that happened, we can look at it with fresh eyes and learn from it.

You'll even feel better about all the not-so-good bits of your day, knowing that you've assessed them, owned those moments, and made a plan for making changes for the better in the future.

You can access the highs and lows, strategize for the

future, and most importantly, feel good about taking control of the day's events. After all, you may not always feel like you're steering the ship in the moment, but when you take accountability for your day and find the hidden lessons and silver lining, this becomes your chance to get back behind the wheel.

Taking inventory of your day can actually feel good once you learn how to make it a habitual practice. You no longer just slide from one day into the next with no idea of how you got there!

So before you settle into too much of a groove in this last part of your day, remember to "run the tape"!

ACTION ITEM #12: TOMORROW, WHEN YOU FIND YOURSELF EASING INTO THE FINAL PORTION OF YOUR DAY, TAKE A MOMENT TO PAUSE—BREATHE—AND RUN THE TAPE, TAKING IT ALL IN, PLAY BY PLAY.

Ask yourself some key questions along the way. You'll be amazed at just how valuable and validating everything you learn, from that brief "rewind," can be.

HABIT 13

PRACTICE GRATITUDE

"I believe you should focus your life on observing the little things, because one day you look back and realize they were the big things."

—Jay Shetty

I don't take anything for granted. Not ever.

I have learned over time to recognize and appreciate the tremendous points of good fortune I've had in my life. I was born to good, loving, and inspiring parents who uprooted their family and left behind everything they knew to move my siblings and me to where they felt our greatest opportunities lay. Their early sacrifices and all the blessings that this afforded me later on are a core source of gratitude for me, and I often reflect on this.

Not everyone is lucky enough to have these early blessings,

and for some, external factors will have them at a disadvantage from the get-go. I consider the war happening in the Ukraine. It's unthinkable—heartbreaking doesn't even begin to cover it. Everyday people—children, parents, whole families—have lost everything through no fault of their own. Innocent people on both sides are paying the price for the indefensible choices of those in power.

Now more than ever, I recognize how my early blessings, like the selflessness of immigrant parents willing to do anything for their family, have helped shape me into the person I am today. And it's taught me that gratitude must be treated like a practice—it needs to be considered and reflected on and then put into some kind of return action or gesture.

Gratitude is not automatic. It is a choice. And it's one you have to consciously make—daily.

Isn't it funny that so many people seem to be *waiting* to be grateful? They're all just working away, inching toward their goals and dreams, all the while thinking that once they have everything they've ever hoped for, *then* the gratitude will come.

I'm sorry to tell you, but this is not reality. Gratitude is not a feeling that just appears once we achieve our goals—like some kind of reward for success that reminds you of all the good things in your life. If you look at it this way, you'll only grow tired of waiting for something that may never materialize.

Gratitude is a conscious practice, and I recommend it as a daily habit—another one that takes work and effort. You have to make the time in your day to take pause and tap into these feelings, *especially* on the days when you're struggling the most. This may sound like the hard part, but it's also the good news: the ability to express gratitude is not a birthright or a personality trait.

Gratitude is an attitude you choose to adopt, develop, and grow.

We are all capable of being grateful; it's not on reserve for just a select few. Even so, the reality is that gratitude comes more easily for some people than others. And there's no shame in discovering that you don't have a naturally grateful disposition (yet!) just as long as you recognize that this is an area of your daily life that you could put more effort into.

And FYI: you're not alone. The fact that there are so many how-to articles and even whole books written about gratitude suggests that we're all working on this. Sometimes it's simply a matter of forgetting to factor gratitude into our daily lives. But sometimes we fail to acknowledge just how necessary this is as a puzzle piece for our day. It is 100 percent necessary, especially in challenging times, when the uncontrollable happens. No one is exempt from life's curveballs. Trust me; it's when the chips are down that you'll want to have points of gratitude to stay focused on, to help keep you afloat and positive.

You might be asking yourself, *Why? Why does it matter if I stop and tap into my gratitude every day or not?*

Well, let me first ask you a question: Why do we do whatever we do, every day and all day? What's one core, universal reason we all keep going, day in and day out?

Happiness.

We do what we do for ourselves, and for the people we love, in pursuit of happiness and with the goal of turning our dreams into reality.

I think about the early days of my career, when it seemed I had everything to lose and no guarantees that anything I was doing would work out. I was hopeful, sure, and hardworking, of course, but one ingredient in the mix that I could not have done without was gratitude. I was thankful every day that after so many major life changes, including a traumatic divorce, that I got a second chance to get myself back on track. After losing my house and having to move my kids three times in a single year, I felt like such a failure, as the insurmountable pressure of responsibility weighed on me, feeling desperate to ensure the stability and well-being of my children. But even through the lowest lows, I held on to such a sense of gratitude for the fact that, with my children in my corner, I wasn't alone. Even on the worst days, when it seemed like the fog just wouldn't lift, I was grateful beyond measure that I had the gift of my children, who became my beacons of light. It was my dedication to being responsible for them that helped me find opportunities that I might not have otherwise been able to spot.

I recall, shortly after the third move (post divorce) with my kids, feeling one of my lowest lows. We had barely just settled into our rental unit, when the landlord advised me he was going to sell. *No, please. Not another move for my kids. Not again.* I can still feel the panic rising up in my chest like it did in that moment. I felt like a loser. I was gutted. But I regained my composure and began thinking of a solution. It wasn't an easy shift to make, mentally, but when the lives and stability of the people you love are at stake, you find the inner strength to push through. I focused on the situation in front of me. I didn't want to move my family again, but this unit was about to be up for sale. So I brainstormed on how I might be able to buy it. With no money, the solution wasn't exactly clear, but I knew I had nothing to lose by coming up with a strategy and pitch. I spoke with the landlord and thanked him for the opportunity to live there, even if it had only been briefly, given his plans to sell. I asked him, given that my family and I were already settled in, if I came up with financial terms that would make buying the unit feasible on my end, would he consider it?

He might have laughed in my face. He might have said *no* flat out. But I owed it to my children to find a way to make this work. And I firmly believe that my sincere approach to the situation with gratitude and a clear plan for his consideration made the difference that day.

I recognize that not everyone feels they have people in their corner, and as hard as that may be, you can be grateful for yourself as your own biggest cheerleader. Self-gratitude is a great place to start.

I remember watching the film *Silver Linings Playbook*, which focused on two main characters, played by Bradley Cooper (as Pat) and Jennifer Lawrence (as Tiffany). Each was struggling with the weight of something devastating—Tiffany with her depression and Pat with bipolar disorder. In one especially moving scene, Pat shares his "belief" about life, one that he learned during his time in the hospital. He shares that, ultimately, you have to do whatever it takes, working your hardest and staying positive along the way, if you really want a shot at the "silver lining." Dedication, effort, and hope—that's what I understood here.

That's how I feel about gratitude. It's that silver lining in the fog—something positive, something you look to and hold on to that nourishes seeds of hope for better days ahead. And it's through channeling gratitude that we are able to achieve and build up our happiness. Author Melody Beattie said that gratitude "turns what we have into enough, and more. It turns denial into acceptance, chaos into order, confusion into clarity . . . it makes sense of our past, brings peace for today, and creates a vision for tomorrow."

As we've already discussed, it can be especially hard to find gratitude in this age of social media. We scroll through all those glossy, happy images, and we lose sight of the fact that not everything is as perfect as it's presented. We subconsciously absorb the visuals and lifestyles being presented to us as "fact," and we hold ourselves up to impossible standards. And while some people are able to internalize what they're seeing and feel inspired, and even motivated, by the glitz and glam, many people just end up feeling like their own lives simply don't measure up.

Instead of feeling discouraged or diminished in our own lives, we need to remember that not everything is always as it seems and that gratitude can give us more power than photos and hashtags. When we look for gratitude as part of our daily self-reflection, we gain a sense of control, and we minimize room for regret. We channel our focus onto all of the positive things we have going on in our lives, and from that perspective, we are able to harness the optimism and motivation we need each and every day.

Gratitude is actually a universal *need* too. When people ask what we are grateful for, we all seem to come up with the obvious answers: our health, our family, a roof over our heads. Yes, yes, yes. All great things! But gratitude can also be highly personal and individual when we dig a little deeper and unearth some of our greatest "little victories."

Oprah Winfrey said, "Gratitude is the child of intention," and in an article for *O Magazine*, readers were asked to share what they were grateful for in 2020. They responded by sharing a variety of personal things on a wide spectrum: the unconditional love of a beloved pet, the insulin pump and miracle of modern medicine that kept a woman's young daughter alive, the regenerative experience of a walk in the outdoors. Their answers were all across the board and even included gratitude for what was hailed as "one of the greatest wardrobe inventions of all time": SPANX.

There really are limitless things in each 24-hour stretch that give us joy—both big and little. We may not stop and reflect on them often enough, but we'd notice if they were missing. And we'd probably also be much more aware of the things we have, and what we could be grateful for, if we were dealt an even harsher hand of cards.

Somewhere today, someone is undergoing their last

chemotherapy treatment. Another patient on a waiting list has just been given the green light for that transplant they've been praying for. A young girl with alopecia is trying on a beautiful hairpiece for the first time. All over the world, every day, people are navigating things we can't imagine. I like to think that if some of these people are managing to keep their spirits up in even the most unimaginable circumstances, we can all find some gratitude within ourselves too. Come on, people! You know this to be true.

Of course, it's not always easy to find that positive headspace even if we're not facing serious health or other life-threatening issues. Coming off the last few years and weathering unprecedented times, most of us can agree it became a lot harder to find gratitude. The world became a very unstable place with the pandemic, economic fallout, political dissention, and even outright war. There still is an enormous amount of hardship happening out there, and bouncing back from so much upset and uncertainty doesn't happen overnight.

But—and this is a big one—there is still *so much* good to focus on! Children will be born; people will get married; someone will say, "I love you" for the first time; someone will get that loan to pursue their dream job. And hey, that barista at Starbucks might finally get your name right on the cup. Yes, the little things do count—and they add up!

And while it can feel a little weird to celebrate our own victories, big and small, when so many people are facing horrible hardships, we have to. The world we live in will never be perfect. Unfortunately, there will always be pain and struggles.

And while we should never ignore others' suffering, we need to find a way to channel it into productive forms of support we can lend, instead of absorbing all that pain ourselves and living in that space. We must not stop living, and we can't stop celebrating life. Because tomorrow brings another day!

One trick when you find yourself struggling to find gratitude is to try getting outside of your own head and doing something in service to *others*. Sometimes, when we engage compassionately in community service, we can get better insight into the blessings within our own lives that we might be taking for granted. So go volunteer at your local community center or help fundraise for a cause you care about—whatever you can do along these lines is going to help you recognize just how blessed you are, every day.

Good fortune, in any capacity, is so much more fulfilling when shared. It's no fun enjoying the blessings of your life alone! Consider the last time you hosted friends or loved ones. When you open your doors to others, what you're really doing is opening your heart. You're inviting people in so that you can share what you have to offer and give back in some way, whether it's through the meal you've cooked or the time and energy you're giving. At the bare bones of it, you're taking your gratitude for all you have and offering to share it with others. This is gratitude in action. And while it's so fulfilling to spend time with the people closest to us and acknowledge how grateful we are for them with gestures like this, it can be equally satisfying to put our energy and gratitude into acts of kindness for those who may not have anyone else.

Giving back to those in need has always been part of the

fabric of who I am. My philanthropic work hasn't just translated into checks handed over; I've devoted much of my time, my energy, and my heart because of my desire to be part of positive change and impact in my community.

I've always considered women and children to be the most vulnerable in our society, and much of my philanthropy has been geared toward supporting this sector of need. For several years, I served as capital campaign chair for one organization in particular, and we were able to raise significant funds and assist in opening a secondary shelter location to support the cause of women and children impacted by domestic violence.

I will never forget the day a woman, affected by my efforts for this foundation, came into my office building. I can still see her, standing at my office door, her young son at her side. She had wanted to come in and thank me, telling me, with tears in her eyes (and mine as well, as soon as she started to speak), that I had helped to change her and her son's life. I was absolutely speechless. It was the briefest moment but had an everlasting impact on my life. No words can ever express what I felt to see this woman and her son, essentially strangers to me, and hear their words of gratitude. In the end, I felt the most gratitude that day, to know that I had been able to make a difference in this family's life. The feeling was as indescribable then as it is now, but that moment will stay with me forever.

Charitable support is a great thing, but giving back with gratitude isn't always about donating time or money to an organized cause. It can be as simple as lending your ear to someone in need. Those of us who are fortunate enough to have a solid support system often take for granted just what it means to have someone check in on us or offer to help us without our having to ask. A wise friend to give advice. A handy neighbor to pop over and help with that sudden leak. A parent to still worry about us, even if it sometimes feels suffocating and makes us bristle. They do it because they love us, not because they must. These support beams are so fixed in our lives that we forget to consider what it might be like to wake up one day and not have them there.

So call someone you know is going through a hard time. Send flowers to your mother just because. Plan a lunch date with your sibling. Pay for the coffee of the person behind you in line, or help that elderly neighbor shovel snow off their driveway, or commit an hour to some volunteer work on the weekend. Heck, even if you just smile at someone and ask them how their day is, you can improve their day and spark your own inner gratitude along the way.

Start today, because your blessings in life are not guaranteed and because they won't always come in the ways you hope or pray for them. I speak from experience; my life's journey so far has been such a roller coaster, and there have been days when I honestly thought I'd seen it all, from emotional despair to financial hardship. My blessings have often been disguised as challenges and have been hard to spot, but I now know that the more you practice gratitude, the better able you'll be to recognize your own hidden blessings down the road.

The last few years especially have taught me that life truly is unpredictable, providing me with a lot of tales to tell. But I've always come out the other side feeling grateful for the lessons learned. In these times of uncertainty, keeping my momentum going with my work and the things—and people—that fueled me is what kept me feeling sane and grounded.

But this is how life goes. Everything can change on a dime, and that's why every single day, and every single moment, matters. If you're still not sold on the benefits of a grateful attitude and heart, consider this:

When you keep gratitude top of mind each day and work from a place of optimism and positivity, you attract and engage other people at that level and establish a kind of positive energy loop amongst yourself and the people around you. The power of attraction is a real thing, and living a life in gratitude will manifest even more blessings. As Oprah Winfrey said, you need to be "thankful for what you have [because] you'll end up having more."

Remember: it's not possible to simultaneously feel both grateful and miserable, or to reflect on the good in your life while feeling bad, so focusing on the good will prevent you from dwelling on the bad and letting yourself sink into a "poor me" bottomless pit. Only one of these thought processes is going to work in your favor. Choose wisely!

Gratitude in action is not only about mastering it as a daily habit. It's about taking it a step farther by channeling it into action *throughout* each day. This could mean being grateful for your family and channeling that into being present with them and cherishing that time. It could be about being grateful for your health and channeling that into making healthy choices about nutrition and fitness. It could mean being grateful for your community and lending a helping hand.

You can also turn gratitude into a daily habit by incorporating it into your daily time of self-reflection. Finish your review of the day with mindfulness of the things you are thankful for, big and small, and brainstorm at least one actionable step you can take tomorrow to make someone feel appreciated or recognized. And don't forget: often the most fulfilling gestures of gratitude are reflected in the time and energy we give to others. So, if you can, why not carve out a few minutes to pass on those feelings of thankfulness and check in with someone you know is struggling?

With so many things to pick at and complain about in the world, it's more important than ever to choose to see the small miracles hidden in your life in each day. Decide right here and right now that you are done dwelling on the things you can't control.

ACTION ITEM #13: START PRACTICING YOUR GRATITUDE TODAY.

Identify those people and things you have been taking for granted. And never forget: the things you take for granted now are the same things someone else will go to bed tonight praying for.

HABIT 14

TAKE CARE OF YOURSELF

"The most important relationship is the one you have with yourself."

—Diane von Furstenberg

Would you believe me if I told you that at least one person a day walks into my office and starts the conversation with "Vivian, I am *stressed out*"?

To be honest, the only stretch here would be to say it's just *one* person a day!

I get it. Business can get chaotic; personal issues don't come with a "pause button," and life in general comes at you fast, day in and day out. But I also think we've become way too conditioned to using the word *stress* as a substitute for more productive language.

For example, we pull an all-nighter working, jump into our

next day, running on caffeine and fumes, and, struggling to put one foot in front of the other without getting agitated, we assume we're simply "stressed." But in this case, if we'd just take a second to reevaluate the underlying reasons why we're feeling the way we are—i.e., lack of sleep—we'd be able to identify exhaustion as our real issue. We'd have a reason, an understanding of why, and we'd be able to make a plan to correct it before this day rolls into the next one.

This isn't to say you're wrong for feeling stress. But okay, you're feeling it, so now what? Are you willing to just accept it as a fixed element in your everyday life? Come on—you deserve better!

The point is this: if you're feeling stressed regularly, and it's become a part of your daily narrative, then clearly, something's gotta give!

The results of a 2019 survey conducted by Everyday Health showed that one-third of participants who visited the doctor did so because of something stress related, and 57 percent of those people reported that they felt "paralyzed" by stress. And while the concept of stress is vast and hugely complex, ranging in severity and covering a massive spectrum of associated variables, let's keep it simple here and talk about good old-fashioned "everyday stress."

How much of a factor is stress in your daily life?

We all live different lives, but one thing most of us have in common is that we face some sort of stress every day. And it can paralyze you. Or it can fuel you, but turning your stress into something productive is easier said than done. I'm not about to tell you that the things keeping you up at night can all be transformed into something productive, because that's not necessarily true. But what I do know is that stress, including the kind caused by our own inner voices trying to get a message through, can be *managed*. The key to effective stress management, like everything else we've talked about so far, is addressing it daily! And the best way to do that is through physical and mental *self-care*.

Sounds pretty simple, right?

So why do we have such a hard time incorporating this into our daily lives? We do so much for others every single day. We look after family; we commit to favors for friends; we extend ourselves to help colleagues—and when it's all said and done, we're the last ones down the list and there's no energy left to help ourselves. This is not a sustainable way to live, and you're not doing yourself any favors by continuing to put yourself last. You cannot pour from an empty cup.

But looking after our own needs is not always easy. There's nothing more relatable than the feeling of being "too busy" to take time out for yourself. And while some of the reasons we ignore our personal needs are common, everyday reasons, people also face bigger issues that involve major life shifts and disruptions. Consider a person who's recently gone through a loss or separation and is now a single parent. I've been there—I get it! Suddenly, your whole life has been shaken up, and you're dealing with an entirely new framework. You feel more pressure than ever to put your kids first, and the concept of "me time" becomes almost laughable. Major shifts come in many forms, be it a change in marital status, financial upsets, or emotional crises—no one is immune to struggle, right? And while I don't believe anyone sets out with the intention of putting themselves last, it's just the natural order of things once we're done putting *everyone else* first.

Beyond the many reasons you might skip self-care, most of which boil down to a lack of time and energy, you may also have a hard time viewing it as a necessity. You might look at taking time out for yourself as more of an indulgence, a rare "treat"—and who has time to do that regularly? Not you! You're busy—you've got places to go, people to take care of, laundry to fold! There's always *something* in the way, right? Some last item on the to-do list, one more email to check . . . and by the time you finally step back and recognize you're completely out of gas, the best option for self-care is sleep. And FYI—sleep is not "self-care"; sleep is a basic necessity of life.

And you and I both know the truth: we don't *feel* good when we don't take care of ourselves. We feel like crap. Period.

Everything is harder and more laborious, and by the end of the day, we're exhausted. And if we do nothing about it today, we're bound to feel worse tomorrow, and the next day, until we get so used to running on fumes that we don't even realize we've totally depleted all our inner resources.

And while you might think the rich and famous are immune to feeling the same pangs of daily stress that we "normal folk" feel, it's just not true. Even the most successful and seemingly put-together celebrities around the world have experienced the dangers of failing to take care of themselves.

When Huffington Post founder Arianna Huffington collapsed in 2007, she realized her collapse stemmed from a never-ending routine that had her burning the candle at both ends. Following her incident, she vowed to make positive, self-care-focused changes to her life. She began making these changes, and has since encouraged others to do the same, with small steps she refers to as "micro-steps" such as breathing exercises, keeping her phone charging in another room while she sleeps, taking a moment to practice gratitude, and working to implement healthy daily habits at the start and end of her days.

Musician and actress Queen Latifah is another big advocate of self-care. She has reported literally having to go away and remove herself from her surroundings to recover from burnout, which she says isn't just a word. "You can be physically exhausted on a cellular level," she said. Her preventative habits include taking the time to check in with herself and paying attention to warning signs, as well as having a support system of friends, family, and even professional resources in place.

In 2019, former First Lady Michelle Obama spoke about why we struggle so much to take care of ourselves. "We are so busy giving and doing for others that we almost feel guilty to take that time out for ourselves." She emphasized the importance of having open conversations about self-care, keeping in mind that we need to take steps now to make sure future generations foster a healthier view of this concept.

No one is immune to burning out. It doesn't matter who you are or what you do for a living; we are all grappling with daily pressures that can really take a toll on our minds and bodies. There is no shame in being open about our stress, and there should be no guilt in putting ourselves first, ideally before the red flags and warning signs show up—and long *before* we hit that wall. We need to recognize and put limits on the cycle of caring for everyone except ourselves. Otherwise, we will continue to push ourselves to our limits in response to short-term demands, draining us to the point where we are barely functioning. This isn't a sustainable approach to healthy living, and it robs us of the reserves we need for more substantial, long-term items.

And even if you don't feel you're on the verge of burnout, taking care of yourself can translate to improved overall wellness and heightened self-awareness, both of which pivot into greater personal confidence and higher levels of productivity. That's why many employers are making it easier and easier to be mindful of the need for better physical and mental health. Consider coffee giant Starbucks, for example. In 2020, in an effort to prioritize the mental health of its employees, Starbucks implemented an annual benefits program offering twenty free sessions with a mental health provider for all US partners and eligible family members.

What is keeping *you* from taking better care of yourself? There's only one barrier: *you!*

There's no shame in finding yourself guilty of this. A lot of men and women feel that tuning into their own needs and prioritizing forms of self-care might reflect some kind of weakness or vulnerability. But let me tell you this: if you don't take care of you, you simply won't have anything left to give to the care of the people you love. So take the steps to make this important change—if not for yourself, then for the people you want to give the best of yourself to.

While everybody's needs are different, and everyone has different resources in terms of both finances and available time, the beauty of self-care is that it does not have to be time-consuming and costly. It can be whatever you need it to be. And you know what? You can get creative with it! My only absolute recommendation is that you implement a daily self-care habit.

This is *your* time. So what if you've only got five minutes to spare? Drop down for a quick stretch and enjoy focusing on your movement. Do you have ten minutes? Tune into a podcast about a topic that interests you to give your brain a quick flex. Twenty minutes? Make a cup of tea or coffee and find a spot to just sit and sip and—*ahhh*—pause and breathe. Once you start focusing on making self-care happen, all sorts of ways to spend that time will come to you. Just go with whatever feels right in the moment, as long as the focus is on you.

Many people have found that, in addition to all the typical self-care routines like massage and meditation, the online world has a lot to offer. Back in 2011, a mysterious web page, www.donothingfor2minutes.com, cropped up online. It displayed a peaceful sunset-over-water backdrop and offered the sounds of gently crashing waves. As soon as you landed on the page, the word "calm" was just visible in a subtle script in the upper lefthand corner of the screen. In the center of the screen, a small countdown timer would begin with the instruction *Do nothing for two minutes.* At the bottom of the screen was another instruction: *Just relax and listen to the waves. Don't touch your mouse or keyboard.*

If you did touch your keyboard or mouse before the two minutes ran out, the timer would flash red, reset, and start the two-minute countdown all over again. The task seemed simple: do nothing for two minutes. And yet, you can imagine how people struggled! Two minutes is a long time when you're asked not to fidget with your mouse or tap, tap, tap at your keyboard.

Those who managed to stick it out for the full two minutes would then be prompted to register their email for more information to come.

Within two weeks of its launch, more than one hundred thousand people had registered without knowing what they were signing up for. And a few months after that, a new website was unveiled: Calm.com. Yep, *that* Calm.

Initially, the site was marketed as a tool designed to help manage the stress felt by Silicon Valley developers, but it wasn't long before the website expanded its audience, and by 2019 the company's revenues had grown to $150 million. I think it's safe to say that cofounders Alex Tew and Michael Acton Smith tapped into something special here: people needed more ways to decompress.

Then, when the pandemic hit in early 2020, the need for self-care became more apparent than ever, in part because we all felt a loss of control over our daily routines. Did you ever think you'd see the day when your grocery run would involve scavenging the city for toilet paper? Had you ever imagined you'd be told when and where you could go—or even whether you could leave your house?

As the pandemic wore on, I sensed the panic rising within me—and the fear and uncertainty for the people I loved and cared about. I also recognized that holding on to this sense of dread wasn't the answer. I had to take care of myself. As we discussed earlier, we can make all the plans in the world, but sometimes we have to pivot directions, and the pandemic forced me to do that when it came to a lot of my habits, including self-care. In some ways, I had to think outside the box. And when I did, I realized I could take care of myself by choosing to focus on the things I could control—specifically, my reactions and my mindset.

When people asked me, "How are you doing with all of this?" my answer was that I kept it moving! Safely and with every precaution in mind, obviously—but moving forward always! I went about my days, no matter how much disruption the virus caused, in a forward direction. I needed to lead by example, and my determination to keep it going and find new ways to adapt let those around me feed off my confidence and follow suit.

When I found myself feeling overwhelmed by the circumstances of the day, I would reflect on stories I had heard from my parents, of their time in Italy during the Second World War. In 1944, they experienced the horrors of war in the city of Cassino, where they both lived: never-ending, piercing sirens and bombs that left the streets ravaged, their homes destroyed, my mother at one point being separated from her siblings, some of them eventually reconnecting and taking shelter for some time in a cave along a hillside. Nursing an injury to her back incurred during their escape, my mother and her family spent three months living in that barren cave, scrounging for food and supplies to bring back to their makeshift home, clinging to their hope and to each other. I thought about my parents, and my relatives who were affected by these unthinkable circumstances, and I found so much strength in knowing that we all come from people who have survived something, and we, too, can survive.

When I asked my parents how *they* were feeling in this new age of uncertainty, with the pandemic causing so much chaos in the world, they told me that this, too, was another war to survive, but the difference this time around was having an enemy you could not see.

Their strength and ongoing resilience are an inspiration to me and a daily reminder of the power in tapping into our gratitude and positivity daily—and finding strength there.

I've come to think of my positive attitude as a habit—just another behavior I tune into as a constant tool and resource at my disposal. It hasn't always been easy, obviously, but I did it—and still do it—for myself and for the sake of everyone around me, determined never to sink under the weight of the "bad stuff." We're all allowed to have bad moments, bad days, rough weeks—the works. That's just life! But we need to make sure those rough patches and unpleasant feelings are the exception, not the rule. Bouts of unhappiness are natural, but those feelings should just be a place you visit, not the mental space you live in. Being miserable can become a habitual attitude, so it's critical that we actively choose to be positive.

And, finally, my daily self-care habits included an emphasis on productivity, staying active, and keeping things as light as possible. We can't ever lose the ability to laugh at ourselves; life can get tough, but we can't take it so seriously *all the time*. We have to find the humor and let ourselves laugh off the stress every now and then!

Before the pandemic, self-care was prescribed as something good to do, but now it's more than that.

Self-care is a nonnegotiable survival skill.

It's like they say aboard airplanes during the flight attendant's safety speech before takeoff: in the event of an emergency, put your own oxygen mask on before you help the person next to you. Why? Because if a lack of oxygen knocks you unconscious, you'll be of no use to yourself *or* the person seated beside you. Self-care is not trivial or selfish; it might actually be the most critical tool you can use to become the healthiest and happiest version of yourself.

ACTION ITEM #14: IDENTIFY SOME DAILY SELF-CARE HABITS THAT YOU CAN IMPLEMENT EASILY ON ANY GIVEN DAY.

Take a moment each day and find some quiet in the middle of all the chaos. Pause. Exhale. Trust me when I tell you this: it is pretty easy to spot the people who are making their physical, emotional, and psychological well-being a priority and to distinguish them from those who are just ready and willing to board the misery train!

HABIT 15

GET SOME SLEEP

"Discover the great ideas that lie inside you by discovering the power of sleep."

—Arianna Huffington

Slip into something comfy, pull those sheets up, and settle in, because it's time for us to talk about sleep.

Once upon a time, in business and in life, people wore their exhaustion like a badge of honor.

Back then, not too long ago, really, it was unthinkable to prioritize sleep because it made you look like an underachiever, or even lazy. *Who has time to sleep?* Sleep, as it was viewed then, was for the weak. It was for people who lacked drive. Bags under the eyes? Just proof that you're getting things done! It was almost considered a point of bragging rights to be the person in the office running on the least amount of sleep because it implied you were busy, and therefore, successful.

Thankfully, the narrative on sleep culture has shifted—in a big way. The core theme now is the opposite: sleep is a must. And it's a major underlying factor in how successful your "waking life" will be. Think about it: if "successful days" are a reflection of your physical, emotional, and mental health, and all of these things are massively affected by your sleep patterns . . . well, it's not hard to see the logic. The relationship between sleep and conscious productivity is undeniable. When you prioritize it, sleep can give you an edge for the day ahead; in fact, it can be a game changer. It's all about listening to your body and giving it what it needs.

And listen up, because your body talks!

When you're hungry, you can feel the deep growl of an empty belly. When you're anxious, you can sense those butterflies flapping their wings in the pit of your stomach. And when you're tired, those heavy eyelids and endless yawns are just more channels of communication your body uses to send you a message. And when you get so tired that you're running on empty, your body will definitely let you know, sometimes delivering messages in ways you won't like—and can't miss.

Running on a lack of sleep is, first and foremost, bad for your brain. You're less able to concentrate, solve problems, or reason your way through tasks, and you wind up feeling forgetful and significantly less productive. Your mood and energy levels are also affected by your sleep, or lack thereof, and irritability is a common consequence of sleep deprivation. You'll also be susceptible to reduced cognitive ability, which impacts your motor skills, leading to slower reflexes and reaction times and making you more vulnerable to accidents and injuries.

I can always spot someone who isn't getting enough sleep. It's in their glassy eyes, their slower response times, and even in how they carry themselves. There's no hiding it.

Lack of sleep also results in all sorts of serious short- and long-term health issues:

- Premature aging
- Cardiac issues
- High blood pressure
- Stroke
- Diabetes
- Depression
- Weakened immune system

And while it may not rank as critical as some of the above life-threatening matters, a lack of sleep is also a sex-drive killer! In a nutshell, it's all bad. There is literally zero benefit to bad sleep habits. None.

Let's circle back to the act of waking up earlier. This is easier said than done, right? For most of us, if asked, we'd say we struggle with getting up because we went to bed late or had "bad sleep." This means we've allowed our evenings to dictate our mornings and thereby to determine the energy level for our day. Unfortunately, this leads to an unhealthy cycle and, ultimately, we wind up exhausted and running on fumes.

The National Sleep Foundation recommends that people between the ages of twenty-six and sixty-four should get seven to nine hours of sleep per night.

Let that sink in for a moment. Seven to nine hours. Per night. Every night.

You have 24 hours in a day, and you should be spending approximately one-third of it asleep. Most of us just can't meet that quota, partly because we have an especially difficult time just winding down and falling asleep as family matters, work pressures, and all the other thoughts that pop up in our minds get in the way.

But does quantity matter? Does it make more sense to base your sleep cycle on how you *feel* each day? If you get a solid six hours and wake up feeling rested and energized, should it matter that you didn't quite hit the NSF-suggested mark?

Taking it one step farther, how sold are you on the idea that the answer to *better* sleep is *more sleep*? I mean, if you're getting plenty of sleep but you still wake up feeling as though you've just been hit by a bus, stretching only to reach that snooze button on your phone, is it really the *amount* of sleep that's the problem here? Or is it the quality?

In my experience, quality is key. Whether you get your full set of hours at night or find a combination of sleep and "restful moments" throughout the day (I'm not a napper myself, though I know some people swear by it), the point is that your body and mind are responding positively, so you're doing it right. And you're the one responsible for how you spend your time—even, and especially, the time you spend asleep.

So don't worry too much about statistics and expert recommendations, and don't be too hard on yourself. You're doing your best, and the fact that this book is in your hands is proof-positive that you're being proactive and trying to make improvements. The most important thing you can do right now is to be mindful of your sleep patterns so that you can positively change them if necessary and then to find what works for you.

When you shift your perspective in this way, you'll stop focusing on "more sleep" and instead shift your focus on reaping the benefits of *more time* in the mornings. It's the cyclical loop of benefits that you're going to get hooked on. This new mindset, one that puts the highest value on added time, is the one that's going to put you on the path to mastering not only your sleep and mornings, but your whole day ahead.

And to do that, you need adequate sleep so your brain can take a break and recharge. Without this downtime, you are essentially refusing your brain what it needs. And when you deny yourself this basic human need for just 24 hours, your ability to function is equal to what you'd be like if you had a blood-alcohol level of 0.10 percent, which, for the record, is over the legal limit for driving. And if you miss forty-eight hours of sleep, you've entered a state of extreme sleep deprivation. At this point, you can expect increased stress and fatigue, but hallucinations are also possible. Obviously, your response times and reflexes will suffer greatly as your body and mind struggle to keep going, and beyond this point, you can safely assume your symptoms of sleep deprivation will get significantly worse, not to mention dangerous.

In the short term, a lack of sleep is going to make you slower in your mind and on your feet, forgetful, irritable, and significantly less productive. In the long term, it's going to make you sick—in one or multiple ways. This is a given. These are the facts. So, now that you know better, let's do better and get ahead of all that!

In Arianna Huffington's bestseller *The Sleep Revolution,* she writes about her collapse from exhaustion, noting that running on empty led her to be the "worst version" of herself. Insisting that "sleep can change your life," she thinks of it as a "performance-enhancement tool." In fact, the entrepreneur and mother of two is firm on the fact that her greatest professional success was achieved only *after* she began to take care of herself. It was her newfound dedication to self-care that triggered the most creative, productive, and happy version of herself.

As part of her daily self-care regimen, she avoids using electronic devices thirty minutes before bedtime, changes into sleep clothes, and creates a space that's conducive to the best possible sleep, every single night.

Okay, I can see you rolling your eyes. No devices before bed? A Zen-like space set aside just for sleep? I know that just isn't possible for some of us, and that for many, your "sleep space" may in reality be a bedroom that's also a rotating door for your kids. And I'm sure, for all the rest of Huffington's sleep strategies, there will be someone out there with a (legitimate) reason why that just won't work for them. But that's not the point.

The key to remember here is that sleep, like self-care, is

nonnegotiable. You need it. You cannot function without it. So do your best. Progress over perfection!

And let me add my own two cents: I suggest skipping that glass of wine (or whatever) before bed. Studies have shown that ingesting alcohol before tucking in can disrupt sleep, cause insomnia, and lead to feelings of increased tiredness the next day. In fact, that feeling of tiredness peaks each day at 2:00 a.m. and 2:00 p.m., even for those who don't drink before bed, but it can be exacerbated by alcohol. This is why people find they feel less energized or "hit the wall" in the middle of the day, and it's also why it is so important to fuel your body with healthy foods to boost your energy and keep you on track!

Remember: your sleep life and your waking life are interconnected, so making quality sleep a daily priority will massively influence the kind of days you'll have.

ACTION ITEM #15: EXPERIMENT WITH DIFFERENT APPROACHES TO IMPROVE YOUR SLEEP.

Maybe you can try going to bed fifteen minutes earlier. Maybe you can have a warm glass of milk or sip a cup of chamomile tea before tucking in. Or maybe you can slip in some noise-canceling earbuds and tune into a soothing sleep soundscape via an app like Calm. Start with whatever you can and work from there.

FINAL THOUGHTS

"We have two lives, and the second begins when we realize we only have one."

—Confucius

In 2019 I was invited to speak and take part in a guest panel for Tony Robbins's Power of Success event series, held in Toronto.

Outside of my individual stage time, for part of the event I was seated along a panel with powerhouse women such as bestselling authors and entrepreneurs like Rachel Hollis and Molly Bloom.

This day would be a lesson about going with the flow for me. And the lesson began before I even stepped onto stage.

From the get-go, things felt frantic. The driver we'd scheduled ahead of time was running late. At this point, there wouldn't be time to wait or call someone else. I hopped in the car with a few members of my team who would be joining me and drove us to the venue myself.

The event was set to begin at 8:30 a.m., and I'd been scheduled to speak later in the morning, at 11:00 a.m. Even while driving at a slow crawl in heavy traffic, I was still feeling good about our timing.

Watching the clock while stopped in gridlock was pointless—there wasn't anything I could do about the congestion on the roads. So I decided to make use of the time. I steadied my mind and visualized stepping out onto the stage. I considered my keynotes and reflected on my message.

I felt my excitement start to mount. I was ready, and as always, I was looking forward to immersing myself in a space that I knew would be bursting with positive energy!

Finally arriving at our destination and pulling into the parking lot, I saw that there was no question that the turnout for the day was massive. What should have been just a few minutes' drive from the parking entry to the door took forty-five minutes!

Almost immediately it was as if someone hit fast-forward. A rep for the event came running out to my car before we even pulled into a spot, declaring, "There's been a change in schedule, Vivian! You're up first! We need to get your mic on!"

First! As in, now?

Okay, I know I said I felt ready—but there wasn't even time for a quick final check in the mirror?

There was no sense questioning the change. There was no time to *think*, period! That's show business for you, and it was showtime!

It was go-go-go as we rushed from the entrance to the hall

to backstage, and finally—the stage itself! Bright lights and a packed house—the time was now! It felt as though from the car to the stage, I'd been beamed in at the speed of light.

I stepped out onto the stage and opened my arms wide. "Good morning, Toronto!"

The event was a success. I loved my time on stage, and I felt empowered by not only the stories and messages shared by the other guest speakers and panelists, but also the people in the audience. Their enthusiasm and genuine interest were inspiring! That curiosity and deep-rooted desire for growth and positive change! *That's what it's all about,* I thought to myself. *This is how we propel ourselves forward. This is how it's done!*

So the day had started in a bit of a frenzy. Big deal. I was prepared and I *still* had to pivot! That's life. And it turned out to be just the extra kick in the ass I needed that morning to really send my energy into overdrive. Being first on the stage hadn't been part of my original plan, but it turned out to be a blessing in disguise. In rushing out onto the stage, there had been no time to get comfortable and settle into my environment—I had to dive in and trust my instincts. It was my true, authentic self out in front of that audience, and that's what I know resonated with so many of the audience members who connected with me afterward.

And I'll tell you, listening to these other people speak and tell their stories, you really come to realize that we all share a common denominator. And I'm not just talking about my fellow guest speakers, either. The nods from the crowd, the genuine smiles of acknowledgment on their faces; they felt it too. Because the truth of the matter is, nobody has a vertical climb from where they start to where they aspire to be.

It's never a straight shot up to your goals. We may have started from different points and under unique circumstances, but we can all share in the experience of being thrown off course, of coming up against unexpected roadblocks and forks in the road.

The journey of life is full of twists and turns, steps back, and missed exits. This is life. And if it wasn't this way, we wouldn't have much to talk about, would we? Because the real adventure is found along the journey, not on arrival. The journey is where the lessons are. It's where you find out what you're made of and decide who you want to be.

There's a road ahead—long, short; who knows? But there's a path worth charting there and a journey that's all your own to look forward to.

Life is happening right now—so leave your comfort zone behind and dive in.

What you do today matters. What you do tomorrow matters. Every day of your life is a blessing, not a guarantee, and you should treat it with care. You can set long-term goals and aim for the moon, but you need clear and effective daily habits to get there. Looking at it another way, what you do (or don't do) today will either boost or burden your tomorrow.

Let's review some of the key concepts we've discussed about how to save (or make) time, generate or renew energy, and otherwise live according to our true intentions.

Habit 1: Wake up with the birds so that you can enjoy a private relationship with the world and really set the pace for the rest of your day. Remember, own your mornings and you'll own the day!

Habit 2: Map out your route to help you stay on track—but be prepared to take detours.

Habit 3: Embrace your daily rituals, including the small details, to make your day run more smoothly.

Habit 4: Accomplish change by chipping away at old routines and implementing new ones each day.

Habit 5: Discover the life-changing benefits of being true to yourself.

Habit 6: Break your projects down into smaller steps to create a clear and actionable path that is both satisfying and motivating.

Habit 7: Recognize that saying *no* can be your superpower!

Habit 8: Practice the art of being present so that you can take more away from life experiences and contribute more to the world.

Habit 9: Adopt effective communication strategies by using

appropriate nonverbal cues, adjusting pace and listening closely, making careful word choices, and reading the room.

Habit 10: Tap into your greatest energy source—which is inside you.

Habit 11: Invest an appropriate amount of time to managing your social media based on what you want to get out of it.

Habit 12: Take inventory of your day; you never know what hidden lesson might surface and catapult you into your greatest life.

Habit 13: Choose gratitude as an attitude you can adopt, develop, and grow.

Habit 14: Remember that self-care is a nonnegotiable survival skill.

Habit 15: Make quality sleep a priority, which will massively influence the kind of day you'll have.

These fifteen daily essentials have made all the difference in *my* life, and I know they have also had a massive impact in the lives of others. Now it's your turn. A fulfilling daily life awaits. You just have to put the work in—and only YOU can do this. Remember: you only get this one life. And only this one moment, right now, is guaranteed. How will YOU make it count?

We've covered a lot of ground throughout this book. We've talked about habits, behaviors, the power of time—and, I think, a little bit of everything along the way, right? Like I said at the very start, you already have everything you need within you, but I'm hopeful that this book has given you access to ideas, strategies, and tools that will help you kick-start your next steps toward living your best life, each and every day.

I want to thank you for taking this trip with me, from cover to cover. I hope you feel inspired to go forward and take on your next 24 with positivity and purpose. This moment, right now, is a chance for change. As they say, if you were looking for a sign, this is it!

Now is the time to start living your best life.

Mic on, it's showtime!

Live it & love it! XO

AUTHOR'S NOTE

In this book, I have taken inspiration from the knowledge, studies, theories, and ideas of many individuals from varied backgrounds. In each case, I have done my best to give credit to the original source via noted references. In the case of quotes, I understand the frequency with which quotes are often misinterpreted, altered, and misquoted over time, but I have done my best to ensure the accuracy of both the quotes used and sources credited.

We are all a sum of our experiences and exposure, and I hope my own insight, as well as the insight and works of others that I have chosen to include in this text, will prove as helpful to you as it has in my own life.

REFERENCES

HABIT 1:

Miah, R. (n.d.) "66 Good Morning Quotes by Famous People." *The Rich Gets Richer.* Retrieved August 28, 2022, from https://www.therichgetsricher.com/66-good-morning-quotes-by-famous-people/.

Sharma, Robin. *The 5am Club.* (n.d.) Retrieved September 20, 2022, from https://www.robinsharma.com/book/the-5am-club.

HABIT 2:

Rohn, John. Retrieved from https://www.facebook.com/OfficialJimRohn/posts/never-begin-the-day-until-it-is-finished-on-paper-jim-rohn/10153028657235635/.

HABIT 3:

McRaven, Naval Adm. William H. Retrieved from https://news.utexas.edu/2014/05/16/mcraven-urges-graduates-to-find-courage-to-change-the-world/.

McRaven, Naval Adm. William H. (2017.) *"Make Your Bed."* YouTube. https://www.youtube.com/watch?v=GmFwRkl-TTc

Duhigg, Charles. (2014.) *The Power of Habit.* https://charlesduhigg.com/the-power-of-habit/.

Benna, Steven. "This one-minute morning routine can improve your productivity all day long." Insider. Retrieved from https://www.businessinsider.com/morning-routine-to-improve-productivity-2015-7.

Jobs, Steve. YouTube. (January 6, 2014.) YouTube. Retrieved August 28, 2022, from https://www.youtube.com/watch?v=C-kBkuaOYO4.

HABIT 5:

Dyer, Wayne W. (n.d.) Goodreads. Retrieved March 25, 2022, from https://www.goodreads.com/quotes/7141914-you-create-your-thoughts-your-thoughts-create-your-intentions-and.

Hai, Roxanne. (May 15, 2015.) "Being vulnerable about vulnerability: Q&A with Brené Brown." Retrieved September 28, 2020, from https://blog.ted.com/being-vulnerable-about-vulnerability-qa-with-brene-brown/.

Thanh_min. (July 1, 2021.) "The Elephant Rope." *Medium.* Retrieved April 30, 2022, from https://medium.com/motivationapp/the-elephant-rope-c22ee790a226#:~:text=As%20a%20man%20was%20passing%20the%20elephants%2C%20he%20suddenly%20stopped,some%20reason%2C%20they%20did%20not

Eurich, T. (n.d.) "Increase Your Self-Awareness with One Simple Fix." Retrieved September 28, 2020, from https://www.ted.com/talks/tasha_eurich_increase_your_self_awareness_with_one_simple_fix?language=en.

Edelman. (n.d.) "2013 Edelman Trust Barometer Finds a Crisis in Leadership." Retrieved November 7, 2022 from https://www.edelman.com/news-awards/2013-edelman-trust-barometer-finds-crisis-leadership.

HABIT 6:

Frederick, Ben. (February 19, 2013.) "Michael Jordan: 10 Quotes on His Birthday." *The Christian Science Monitor.* Retrieved August 28, 2022, from https://www.csmonitor.com/USA/Sports/2013/0219/Michael-Jordan-10-quotes-from-His-Airness-the-King/On-obstacles#:~:text=On%20obstacles,-Peter%20Jones%2F%20Reuters&text=But%20obstacles%20don't%20have,2%20of%2010.

Boogard, Kat. (2019.) "What's Microproductivity? The Small Habit That Will Lead You to Big Wins." *Trello.* https://blog.trello.com/microproductivity-break-tasks-into-smaller-steps.

Cowan, N. (2010.) "The Magical Mystery Four: How Is Working Memory Capacity Limited, and Why?" *Current Directions in Psychological Science,* 19(1), 51–57. https://doi.org/10.1177/0963721409359277.

HABIT 7:

Clay, Rebecca A. (2013.) "Just Say No." American Psychological Association. https://www.apa.org/gradpsych/2013/11/say-no.

HABIT 8:

Tolle, E. (2004.) *The Power of Now: A Guide to Spiritual Enlightenment.* Namaste Publishing.

Wikipedia Contributors. (February 5, 2019.) "Attention span." Wikipedia; Wikimedia Foundation. https://en.wikipedia.org/wiki/Attention_span.

HABIT 9:

Epictetus. Retrieved November 7, 2022. from https://www.brainyquote.com/quotes/epictetus_106298.

HABIT 11:

Statista Research Department. (September 10, 2021.) "Number of Social Media Users Worldwide." Statista. https://www.statista.com/statistics/278414/number-of-worldwide-social-network-users/#:~:text=How%20many%20people%20use%20social.

(n.d.) "70+ Social Media Statistics you need to know in 2021 [Updated]." https://www.omnicoreagency.com/instagram-statistics/.

Atad, C. (October 6, 2021.) "Anderson Cooper says Instagram 'depresses me:' 'I leave feeling worse than when I got on.'" ET Canada. Retrieved September 20, 2022, from https://etcanada.com/news/825546/anderson-cooper-says-instagram-depresses-me-i-leave-feeling-worse-than-when-i-got-on/.

Smith, K. (December 30, 2019.) "122 Amazing Social Media Statistics and Facts." Brandwatch. https://www.brandwatch.com/blog/amazing-social-media-statistics-and-facts/.

HABIT 12:

Cambridge English Dictionary. (n.d.) Retrieved September 16, 2020, from https://dictionary.cambridge.org/us/dictionary/english/self-reflection.

Browning, G. (November 24, 2014.) "Take a Look Back at Your 2014 Year with These 5 Questions." Retrieved September 17, 2020, from https://www.inc.com/geil-browning/personal-reflection-get-started-with-these-5-questions.html.

Shrestha, Praveen. (November 17, 2017.) "Ebbinghaus Forgetting Curve," in *Psychestudy.* https://www.psychestudy.com/cognitive/memory/ebbinghaus-forgetting-curve.

HABIT 13:

Beattie, Melody. (November 18, 2021.) "Gratitude." Melody Beattie. Retrieved August 28, 2022, from https://melodybeattie.com/gratitude-2/.

Bowler, Kate. (October 14, 2020.) "Here's What O Readers Are Most Thankful for This Year." Oprah Daily. https://www.oprahmag.com/life/a34330280/o-readers-thankful/.

Connolly, M., Slade, M., & Allison Young, M. (2020.) "United States of Stress 2019." Everyday Health. Retrieved November 10, 2020, from https://www.everydayhealth.com/wellness/united-states-of-stress.

HABIT 14:

Morse, B. (June 22, 2021.) "Arianna Huffington: What You Need to Know to Prevent Burnout." Inc.com. Retrieved August 28, 2022, from https://www.inc.com/brit-morse/arianna-huffington-wellbeing-stress-burnout.html.

Copelan, C. (April 4, 2019.) "Queen Latifah Says 'Burnout Is Not Just a Word, It Is Something Physical.'" *Parade.* https://parade.com/865836/ccopelan/queen-latifah-says-burnout-is-not-just-a-word-it-is-something-physical/.

Good Morning America. (n.d.) "Listen to Michelle Obama's Self-Care Message: Why Women Need to Put Themselves First." Retrieved May 1, 2022, from https://www.goodmorningamerica.com/wellness/story/listen-michelle-obamas-care-message-women-put-64189509.

Unidentified. Starbucks Stories. (n.d.) Stories.starbucks.com. Retrieved March 25, 2022, from https://stories.starbucks.com/press/2020/starbucks-transforms-mental-health-benefit-for-us-employees/.

Curry, David. "Calm Revenue and Usage Statistics (2020)." (October 30, 2020.) Retrieved November 24, 2020, from http://www.businessofapps.com/data/calm-statistics/

HABIT 15:

"National Sleep Foundation Recommends New Sleep Times." (n.d.) Retrieved March 25, 2022, from https://els-jbs-prod-cdn.jbs.elsevierhealth.com/pb/assets/raw/Health%20Advance/journals/sleh/NSF_press_release_on_new_sleep_durations_2-2-15.pdf.

CDC. (March 21, 2017.) "Drowsy Driving: Sleep and Sleep Disorders." Retrieved December 17, 2020, from https://www.cdc.gov/sleep/features/drowsy-driving.html.

Umoh, Ruth. (March 12, 2018.) "Arianna Huffington Says She Became Successful After She Quit One Common Bad Habit." Retrieved December 22, 2020, from https://www.cnbc.com/2018/03/11/arianna-huffington-became-successful-after-she-started-sleeping-well.html.

Pacheco, Danielle. (March 11, 2022.) "Alcohol and Sleep." Sleep Foundation. Retrieved May 1, 2022, from https://www.sleepfoundation.org/nutrition/alcohol-and-sleep.

ABOUT THE AUTHOR

Vivian Risi is the president and CEO of one of the largest real estate brokerages in North America. With a career in the industry spanning nearly four decades, Risi is a recognized philanthropist, noted speaker, celebrated leader, and mentor in her field.

After immigrating to Canada at a young age, Risi journeyed from humble beginnings and endured many challenges, which resulted in the hard-earned wisdom that she now shares to inspire others—always leading with the core message: *It's never too late to change the trajectory of your life.*

Based in Toronto, Canada, Risi is also the author of *Yes You Can: It All Starts with You.*